THE STRIPED SHIPS

BY THE SAME AUTHOR

THE STRIPED SHIPS

by
Eloise McGraw

Margaret K. McElderry Books
New York

Maxwell Macmillan Canada
Toronto

Maxwell Macmillan International
New York   Oxford   Singapore   Sydney

Margaret K. McElderry Books
Macmillan Publishing Company
866 Third Avenue
New York, NY 10022

Maxwell Macmillan Canada, Inc.
1200 Eglinton Avenue East
Suite 200
Don Mills, Ontario M3C 3N1

Macmillan Publishing Company is part of the
Maxwell Communication Group of Companies.

First edition
Designed by Nancy B. Williams
Printed in the United States of America
10 9 8 7 6 5 4 3 2 1

Library of Congress Cataloging-in-Publication Data
McGraw, Eloise Jarvis.
The striped ships / by Eloise McGraw. — 1st ed.
p.   cm.
Summary: Juliana, an eleven-year-old Saxon girl, loses her home
and family when the Normans conquer England in 1066 and seeks to
order her life by becoming involved in the creation of the Bayeux
tapestry.
ISBN 0-689-50532-9
1. Great Britain—History—Norman period, 1066–1154—Juvenile
fiction.   [1. Great Britain—History—Norman period, 1066–1154—
Fiction.   2. Bayeux tapestry—Fiction.]   I. Title.
PZ7.M47853St   1991
[Fic]—dc20   91-7729

*To the unknown designer and
anonymous hands that created
the great embroidered hanging known as the
Bayeux Tapestry*

ACKNOWLEDGMENTS

I wish to thank my friend Dr. C. Warren Hollister of the University of California at Santa Barbara, internationally known expert on Anglo-Norman affairs, for his unstinting and invaluable advice, information, maps, and patient answers to hard questions, all through the writing of this book. Thanks, too, to Fr. Hugh Feiss, OSB, or Mount Angel Abbey, Oregon, for his kind and full response, plus a whole packet of information, about very early monastic calendars. My gratitude also goes to longtime friends Julie Baker McLauchlan of Buckinghamshire and Dorothy Clewes of Sussex, the first of whom supplied some wonderful material on Saxon Canterbury, and the second, snapshots and topographical reminders of Rye and Pevensey. Last but certainly not least, my thanks to Mary Norman of the Lake Oswego (Oregon) Public Library, who organized interlibrary loans from far and wide during the first spadework of my research.

A NOTE ON THE DATES
IN THIS BOOK

Alert readers may notice that some of the dates given in this story seem late, according to modern church calendars. For instance, October 14, 1066, the date of the Norman invasion of England, is identified as Michaelmas Eve, which today would fall on September 27.

The explanation is that in the eleventh century, and until the late sixteenth century, both Britain and Christian Europe used the "old style" or Julian calendar, which was based on the calculation of the solar year as 365¼ days. The "new style" or Gregorian calendar was introduced by Pope Gregory XIII in 1582 after astronomers discovered that an eleven-day discrepancy had accumulated between the Julian calendar and the solar year. England nevertheless clung to the old style for another two centuries, and even today there are places which adhere to the old calendar for certain customs or celebrations.

The people of the eleventh century paid less heed than we do to dates and clocks. They measured their lives by the numerous Holy Days and the regular sounding of the bells from some nearby priory or abbey, calling the monks to their devotions. The bells began with nocturns and matins (2:30–3 A.M.), then sounded prime (dawn), then terce (about 9 A.M.), sext (noon), nones (2–3 P.M.), vespers (about 5 P.M.), and finally compline (about 6:30 P.M.). Nearly everybody went to bed shortly after dark.

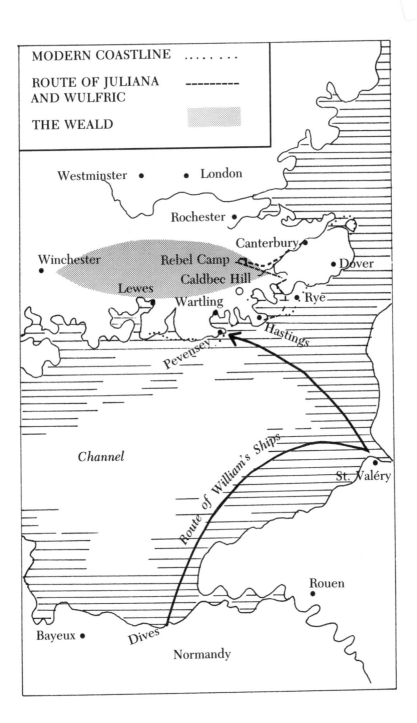

MODERN COASTLINE ....

ROUTE OF JULIANA
AND WULFRIC ----------

THE WEALD

Westminster • • London

Rochester •

Canterbury•

Winchester • Rebel Camp • Dover
Caldbec Hill

Lewes
Wartling • Rye

Hastings

Pevensey

Channel

Route of William's Ships

St. Valéry

Rouen

Bayeux • Dives

Normandy

P R O L O G U E

JULIANA WOKE AND SAT BOLT UPRIGHT IN THE MEAGER pile of straw that was her bed. She had dreamed again that she was back on the stony beach at Pevensey, watching the strange striped ships grow larger and larger through the morning mists. She could feel again the pebbles under her feet, the chill breeze tangling her hair, and see the taut sails—striped, like the ships, in gold and red, gold and black, gold and red and green—more and more of them appearing out of the gray seas that should have been empty, all riding the high of the tide straight toward Pevensey harbor.

And then in the dream she stumbled away across the stones, running, scrambling, crying, "Normans! Normans! *Father!* Normans!" straining her throat, and no sound coming however hard she shrieked. But there she always awoke with pounding heart, fighting off the terror that surged back in the dream's wake to break over her like an evil wave.

She wondered if she would dream that dream the rest of her life. She did not want to think about the rest of her life. The first eleven years of it had ended, as in a thunderclap, the autumn morning of Michaelmas Eve, in the year 1066. Even now, seven nightmare months later, she could not imagine what her future would be like.

1

O N E

THE MORNING OF MICHAELMAS EVE BEGAN FOR JULIANA like many another, with her big brother Sweyn rolling her unceremoniously out of bed by planting his bare foot in the small of her back and shoving hard.

"Up! Up!" he cried over Juliana's indignant protests. "The sun is near rising, my Jilly, and what will he shine on, if not your face? Up, Wulfric, out of that straw now, *out* you go, my little monk! Stop—stop!—remember you're a holy scholar, not a fighting man . . . Eh, stop it!"

Juliana sat a moment, blinking, on the hard oaken floor, rubbing her elbow, as her younger brother Wulfric, propelled out of the wide bed on the opposite side, leaped back in, his eyes still stubbornly tight shut, and began to pummel Sweyn with both fists. Sweyn, shouting with laughter, grabbed one of the pile of bolsters and buried his brother's flailing fists and tousled head under the sack of feathers.

3

By the time Wulfric had fought free, his round face redder than the bolster cover, Juliana had abandoned all thought of sleep and was pulling her linen undertunic over her head. Already the maids and servingmen were clattering and chattering as they bustled about the single great room, flinging open the wooden shutters, renewing the fire in the central hearth, clearing away their sleeping pallets from the benches around the walls. Over in the far corner, the curtains were still drawn around her parents' cupboard-bed, but by the time Juliana had shivered her way into her long woollen kirtle, teeth chattering in the chilly autumn dawn, her father Baldric, Thane of Pevensey, had thrust aside the bed hangings and was shouting for his body-servant. His shock of blond hair, red-tinged, and his ruddy square face set with vivid blue eyes, would have been absurdly like Wulfric's but for his flowing mustache.

One shoe on and the other in her hand, Juliana ran across the Hall and flung herself upon him, tumbling him back against the wedge of bolsters and entangling them both in the bed-curtains. He gave a roar of laughter and defended himself by tickling her; his wife Hildegund sat up, complaining, and fended them off, trying to protect little Ragni, on her other side. Ragni was only three and still slept with her parents. Scolding Juliana for her wild ways and Baldric for encouraging them—as usual without any noticeable effect on either one—Hildegund contrived to hand Ragni over to her nurse, who was leaning into the bed to reach for her. Then the manservant appeared with Baldric's hose and tunic, and the thane arose, his battle-strong arms effortlessly setting aside his lanky daughter.

Juliana wandered over to a bench, laced on her other

shoe, and submitted to having her hair combed by one of the bondsmaids. As the horn comb jerked and yanked its way through her waist-long tangled mop, she sat watching a sparrow that had flown in through the open window and could not find its way out. In and out among the rafters it fluttered—up and up until it disappeared into the dusk and swirling smoke under the steep-pitched roof—down again to swoop from one end of the long Hall to the other. Why could the little creature not see the pale rectangles of the windows, feel the chill air of freedom? *Perhaps it does not want to get out,* thought Juliana. *There are falcons and owls and little cats out there . . .*

But suddenly the angle of the sparrow's flight shifted; it thumped and fluttered against the window's edge, then shot out into the dawn and vanished. At the same moment the far-off sound of the bell ringing for prime in the little priory on the road to Lewes drifted faintly through the open shutters. Juliana jumped up, pushing away bondsmaid and comb together as Nurse Editha waddled over to her from the clothes-chest and slipped her long, round-necked white woollen *rocc* over her head. Hildegund, now fully clad and wearing a golden brooch, hurried after, bringing her a mantle. It was the old blue mantle, nearly outgrown, with embroidery Juliana had worked when she scarce knew which way to hold a needle, and she did not want to wear it.

"I am not cold, Mother!" she protested as she clasped the wide leather girdle about her waist and hitched the *rocc* up over it to reveal a band of the crimson kirtle underneath. "I will not need the *rocc* and a mantle too . . . No, no . . ."

"You will, certainly. Juliana, you must obey your parents.

How often must I . . . *Juliana*, stand quiet so I may . . . Oh, do behave! Nurse . . ."

A pair of firm hands suddenly seized the mantle, pulled it down over Juliana's head and settled it inarguably onto her shoulders. "Now, my Jilly! Try to remember you are a thane's daughter!" commanded Nurse Editha, now Ragni's nurse—once Juliana's and Wulfric's, and before them, Sweyn's. "You must go properly clad to the *burgh* and Lady Edwina."

"Averil and Bernadette are a *king's* thane's daughters—and they will not be wearing mantles! Or if they are, it will be *new* mantles, not old worn-out ones, growing too short!"

"Hush. The weaving-women have not finished the cloth for your new one." The nurse jabbed a long silver pin through the mantle's folds to fasten it. "Now take a morsel of bread with you, and mind you don't linger on the road!"

"And sit up properly in Lady Edwina's presence," fussed Hildegund. "With your feet together, as I have taught you. She will one day be your marriage-mother, remember! And be diligent with your needle, and comport yourself with—"

"Yeh-so, Mother, I will, I will! Good-bye . . ."

Juliana snatched a chunk of bread from the trencher the cook's boy had brought in and had almost reached the door when she stumbled over a sudden obstacle and went reeling. It was Wulfric's outstretched foot, she saw when she whirled about. He was sitting on a bench, the other foot propped beside him, methodically winding the long leathern strips that cross-gartered his linen hose, and regarding her severely.

"You lamed my Elf, you did," he said.

"I didn't, then!"

"You did. Yesterday. You rode him when I said not."

"I only went out to the hill field to watch them harvesting," said Juliana sulkily. "I did him no harm—he stumbled!"

"He doesn't like to gallop fast, Elf doesn't. Not like you and Sweyn. He's old, Jilly. You're not to ride him."

"Only to the *burgh*? This one morning? I'll bring you some more goose quills—"

"Father Cuthbert gives me quills enough. Ride Sweyn's new horse if you want to fly like a bird."

"I will, then! And may your pens split and your ink dry up and Father Cuthbert scold you, and—"

Muttering to ease her conscience—and her wounded feelings, for Wulfric had ever looked to *her*, not Father Cuthbert, to supply his unpredictable needs—Juliana stalked on, turning at the doorway to thrust out her tongue. But Wulfric's attention was again on his gartering. The last she saw of him, he was composedly crossing the last strips precisely below his knee.

A fine chance she had of riding Sweyn's new horse, she was thinking as she stepped out into the morning and ran down the outside stair. Sweyn was a man of sixteen now, and the spicy young stallion their father had given him last week was no gentle hack, but the sort he could ride to a battlefield. It was ill luck he had missed this past summer's foregathering of the thanes and their fighting men. But after all, the Norman invaders had not come; Baldric scoffed that Normans feared the sea. And *next* time King Harold Godwinson summoned the *fyrd*—then Sweyn would ride with them.

Juliana paused a moment, watching Sweyn across the broad expanse of courtyard as he counted sacks of grain, her pride in him tinged with helpless jealousy. She was jealous of his horse, his growing skill with bow and sword, of the life of battles and sudden departures and high adventure that he would share now with their father—while she stayed tamely in Pevensey awaiting her eventual wedding to Lord Alfgar's son Chelric. Sweyn was a man grown, long-legged and flaxen-blond, like their mother Hildegund and her Danish forebears—like Juliana herself—with eyes the clear gray of brook water. They had always been much alike, the two of them, and she cherished him second only to her father.

But she did not waste breath begging to ride his horse.

Instead she headed for the nearest of the outbuildings enclosed by the timbered palisades, peering up to assess the lightening sky, which promised a crisp blue day once the mists had cleared. The courtyard was busy already, for with Michaelmastide came quarter-day. Baldric's many and varied tenants—churls with a score or more acres, poor cottars with one or two, fishermen, shepherds, ironsmiths, huntsmen, bakers, all who lived by their trades—were coming and going through the great open gates to bring their due rents, which they paid in kind. Stacks of firewood, new brooms, sacked grain, a sheep for slaughter and ironware for harness, eels and herrings and ale-jugs and eggs in baskets, cheeses, sesters of honey and salt, hens peering through the woven willow of their crowded coops, were collecting steadily around the barns and sheds, or being carried into the half-underground storerooms beneath the Hall. Old Lustwin, Baldric's reeve, stalked here and there with his talley-board, marking the payments, and Sweyn was helping him. Juliana slipped unnoticed into the stables.

One of the grooms peered out of a stall and came forward hastily, mumbling, "God's greeting, Thane's Daughter."

" 'S greeting. Has Elf gone lame?" she asked anxiously.

The man blinked, shifted his feet, and blurted, "He limps on the left fore."

"Limps only? But is his leg cool?"

"Cool as spring-water! It's his hoof—I dug a stone out yestereve. 'Twas not there at midday, my oath on it! I am a good, careful—"

"Be easy. If he's not lame, that's the end of it!" Relieved, she put Wulfric out of her mind, reminding herself that one day Chelric's bride-gift would make her the owner of ten fine mares. But until then . . . Vowing to tease her father yet again for a mount of some sort—even a pack-pony grown too old for travel—Juliana ran out of the stables and toward the gate.

A glance over her shoulder showed her Baldric just emerging from the Hall, strong and splendid in his best scarlet, with his broad gold armbands ringing his upper arms, which she could not span with her two hands, his legs in their cross-gartered linen as sturdy as tree trunks. He strode toward Lustwin, greeting his tenants, and she hurried on her way unnoticed, into the narrow streets beyond the palisades, absently responding to the repeated "God's blessing, Thane's Daughter," "A good morning,

9

Thane's Daughter," until she had gained the Lewes road and left the town behind. It was a mile's walk along the old Roman way to the *burgh*, and already full light.

The *burgh*—Lord Alfgar's Hall and its stockaded courtyard—was three times the size of Baldric's and boasted many more outbuildings, one of which was a separate sleeping chamber for Lord Alfgar, the King's Thane, and his lady. Otherwise it was much like home. Juliana ran up the outside stair and made her way through the long, busy room to the far end, where a space was kept clear of the servants' cooking and mending and bustling for a group of embroidery frames, at which Averil and Bernadette and three of the maidservants were already at work. Juliana slid breathlessly onto her stool between the thane's two daughters, the sisters of her betrothed, and picked up her needle.

Averil, eldest and ever conscious of it, shot her a reproving glance, but Bernadette, who was only nine, smiled a welcome and whispered, "Jilly, I think we will start the new wall-hanging for the bishop! At least—they have fetched the linen from the weaving shed, so maybe . . . Mother says we are to design it ourselves, one panel apiece!"

"*Ourselves?*" Juliana echoed.

"Following my mother's plan," Averil put in austerely. "My father wishes it to tell of Harold Godwinson, and all the battles my father fought beside him when he was earl—your father, too—and how he was made king."

"And old King Edward's death beforehand, and the great

star afterward," Bernadette added. "The 'long-haired star.' Oh, I was frightened. Jilly, could you draw that star for me to work? With its long, bright tail—"

"It is called a comet," Averil informed her.

"Only by the bishop," retorted Juliana.

Bernadette merely rolled her eyes up and held her tongue.

"I will do my best to draw it," Juliana promised her. "I mind it well," she added with a little shiver. "How bright and strange it was . . ." For seven nights running, last Eastertide, the long-haired star had traveled in silent brilliance across the deep, dark sky. Then—gone. Everyone had been frightened. Well, perhaps not Baldric or Sweyn or Lord Alfgar—or their lord, Harold Godwinson, crowned a bare three months earlier—but everyone else. Clearly, it was a portent. But whether of ill-luck or good for the new king, few could agree, and no one knew.

"Daughter! Juliana! Do you sit idle?" Lady Edwina strolled toward them, her elegant head erect under the draped folds of her long green headrail, her deft hands busy with the drop-spindle. "Persist with your work, my dears. I would like the bolster covers finished today."

So the new hanging must wait, thought Juliana as she reluctantly took up the old embroidering where she had left off.

Think of tomorrow, and the harvest fair, she told herself as she craned her neck to peer out of the window beside her—a little glad after all of the mantle, for the shutters were flung wide, and the air was still cold with the morning mists. Out there, the vast curving sweep of the common fields was striped like a great embroidery with the colors of one man's wheat and the next man's barley, some strips dark with turned earth, others lying fallow, but most scythed and golden, studded with the fresh-garnered shocks of grain. In the distance she could see a line of harvesters still laboring, bent and swaying in the familiar rhythm as they swung their sickles. By evening, someone would cut the last sheaf—no doubt several men together, so the piskies and corn-elves could not place the blame on any one—and the sheaf would be wreathed with flowers, and decked like a maiden, and brought to the feast tomorrow in the market square at Pevensey. A whole cow would be roasted, and sheep and swine, and her father and Lord Alfgar would provide oceans of ale and mead, and every man, woman, and child would make holiday. But first, finish the embroidery. Tiresome, tiresome . . .

It was not really tiresome, she admitted to herself as she reached for a new skein of yarn. It was sometimes bewitching to make flowers and figures grow on the taut linen. It was always amusing to watch Lady Edwina pace back and forth, correcting, instructing, complaining about wasteful cooks and clumsy servants and her aching head and her careless daughters, talking on and on in her placid voice as she moved here and there among the frames, always with a hank of wool hung on her shoulder. And all the while her spindle would be dropping and whirling as her swift fingers twisted the fibers, then leaping up to her hands like a living thing while she wound and looped the spun thread. In truth, Juliana liked these mornings well—especially nowadays when she could feel her needle-skill growing with every stitch.

But today she did not want to sit still. She wished Bernadette had not mentioned the long-haired star.

She did sit, fidgeting—though with her feet dutifully together—for the next two hours, minding her stitches and answering when she was spoken to. Then Lord Alfgar summoned his lady on some matter, and Bernadette tagged along, and a bondsmaid brought the infusion of comfrey to treat Averil's complexion. While no one was looking, Juliana left the Hall. She did not really plan it, but once outdoors—and then somehow across the stockade and out the gates—she could not turn back.

She did not even look back, but ran and leaped and bounded. As the faint notes of the priory's bell drifted across the fields, ringing for terce, she swerved off the road and across ditches and pasture, skirting the town and its houses and making straight for the sea.

The stony beach was empty, save for the shore birds— great gatherings of them, running and stopping, running and stopping on their spindly legs—and the gulls wheeling in wide, silvery flights in and out of the mists, with the sea's uproar almost drowning their shrieking cries. Juliana pulled off her shoes, hitched up her kirtle, and ran, too, wishing she could fly. But the pebbles hurt her bare feet, and she dropped at last in happy exhaustion and lay back, panting . . .

It was then she caught sight of the three striped ships lying offshore in the thinning mist. She sat up, frowning, thinking them King Harold's, but then knowing them to be some other, for the king's fleet had sailed to London, Baldric had said so. And these were not at anchor, but approaching—fast.

13

Abruptly she was on her feet. Three more ships with bellied sails—striped in red, gold, black, green—appeared out of the mist-clouds like phantoms out of the marsh. Behind them, another five or six, strung out—no, eight—ten—a dozen, small in the mid-distance but swiftly looming larger, closer, as they rode the incoming tide.

She whirled and scrambled away across the rocky shore, forgetting her shoes, making for the ruined Roman fort beside the harbor, where she clambered up onto the broken wall to look again. By then the dozen ships had swollen to scores—to hundreds—the nearest ones so close she could see the carved beasts rearing on the tall, curving prows, the fluttering standards, the row of shields glinting along the gunwales, the crowded dark heads behind. She stood transfixed as the first sharp keel grated upon the shore, and a tall man sprang out, stumbled, and recovering, grasped two fistfuls of England to raise high.

Another ship and another beached and tilted steeply among the pebbles, and more men swarmed over the low gunwales to splash shoreward in the shallows, coaxing overwrought horses to leap out after them. And she was so dumbfounded to see live, plunging stallions emerge from longboats that she barely realized how many men were pouring from them, too, until the beach was black with them, the first horsemen already mounted and spurring toward the town, others in pairs, then clusters, then strung-out lines running after on foot—Normans all. She knew them for Normans by their hairless faces and close-cropped heads, shaven halfway up their skulls in back. Frozen with disbelief, she crouched without moving until still more of them bearing timbers and tools started straight up the path to the ruins where she huddled. That wrenched her loose and sent her scrambling away from them along the top of the wall, half-tumbling down from it on the opposite side, crying, "Normans! Normans! *Father!* Normans!" though she was too far from the town to be heard, too late to sound warning of what was already happening.

She ran on, regardless, toward the market square, shrieking warnings to villagers who all seemed to be running the other way, and would not listen or stop. At last she arrived, gasping and bramble-scratched, with bruised feet and aching side, to find the square—garlanded for harvest—now a chaos of Normans and clattering hoofs and foreign shouts, and squeals from the swine they were dragging from the pens and slaughtering right there on the cobbles, along with the harvest-feast cow. Alflaed the harbormaster lay bloody and still on his own doorstep. Rhonwen the bondmaid screamed and screamed. There were few Saxons anywhere, save those struck down and dying, or too old or young to flee, or those trying to hide in the churchyard. And no armed men of the *fyrd* came storming out with their battle axes because there were none, *none,* in Pevensey or in their camps up and down the Sussex coast where they had been all the long summer, waiting, gathered and ready. They were scattered now to their own fields and harvests—even Lord Alfgar's housecarls were busy at the *burgh* on the road to Lewes. Because who would have believed that sea-wary Normans would risk crossing the Channel until spring? Now the Normans were here, and the defenders were not—and where Lord Alfgar and Sweyn and her father were this minute, God alone knew.

Juliana turned toward home to find them, to warn her mother and Wulfric and all the others in the big timbered Hall beyond the square. She saw its palisade and roof-slope—and men running—and at the same moment saw flames bloom like a scarlet flower from the Hall's thatch and angry smoke billow up. Next instant she was clipped by the arm and swung upward, and found herself dangling against a horse's steaming flank, with a voice laughing above her and a stirrup gouging her side. Then she was flung away into a hard pair of arms and downward against the ground with the breath knocked out of her, enveloped in a sour, sweaty stench. Gasping and shoving at the leather-clad body that pinned her, the hands that ripped at her under-tunic, she was conscious of a goat's bleating and someone screeching, a tugging at the weight crushing her, and a voice she knew yelling, "Loose her, loose her, you demon, she's a child only—let her go!"

The weight rolled off, the man in the leathern garment sprang to his feet, drew a short sword, and ran the woman through—and it was Jutta, a cottar's widow. She dropped where she stood, her blood spurting almost to where Juliana's flax-pale dusty hair spilled onto the cobbles, and the Norman kicked Jutta's body aside and grabbed at the goat whose tether she had loosed as she died. Then he was gone, dragging the animal across the square, and Juliana was stumbling, staggering, half-falling in the opposite direction, away from the blood and the flaming Hall, and had no further thought until she reached the marshy edge of Pevensey estuary. There she sank down among the reeds and turned her inner eye away from the sight of Jutta and the man's sword plunging home, and stopped her ears against the sounds from the town.

It was some time later, and she was no longer shaking but stony-hard and stony-still, when the reeds rustled and a small child's face peered through at her—and then a second one, a little higher. "It's the thane's daughter," whispered one to the other. After a moment she knew them. They were Jutta's children, who sometimes brought Jutta's rent-payment of eels or eggs or bilberries to Baldric's Hall.

They had been waiting long, they told Juliana, for their mother to bring the goat. Their mother had said to run ahead here to the water's edge, and wait there until she fetched the goat.

After another moment—for it seemed hard to think, harder to speak—Juliana whispered, "Where did she mean to take you?"

"To our uncle at Wartling-in-the-marshes. He is Grim the salter, her brother. We have a boat yonder."

Juliana stumbled to her feet. "Show me where it is."

They hesitated, then turned and led her through the reeds to the estuary—still full, but sucking at its muddy banks now, because the tide was on the ebb. There was a small scull there, and oars.

"Get in. Make haste," said Juliana.

But now they resisted. "Will we not wait for our mother, and the goat?"

"We will wait for nobody and nothing," Juliana told them,

and lifted the boy into the scull and would have helped his sister after him, but she twisted away, crying that they must wait for their mother.

"Your mother is dead!" Juliana burst out at her, voice harsh and shaking. "The Normans killed her! Mine too, no doubt! Will you stay till they kill us? Get in the boat!"

She pushed the child after her brother, not heeding their blank, shocked faces but stepping blindly into the scull. It rode deep with the three of them, but it floated. She took the oars and shoved off, and began to row.

T W O

NOW, SEVEN MONTHS LATER IN A BLEAKER DAWN, JULIANA awoke with a gasp from the ever-recurring dream of the striped ships. She sat shivering, waiting for the futile cry of "Normans! *Father!* Normans!" to quit echoing in her mind—for the images of the flaming Hall and Jutta to grow dim enough to bear.

Mercifully, they faded, both dream and still-raw memories trailing away like fog into the reality of this chilly daybreak, leaving only a weight of loneliness and anger. Then hunger, ever-present, surged back to the center of her mind. With the damp cold numbing her limbs, she got up stiffly from the corner of the storeroom floor, feeling more like old Elveva, who had forty winters in her joints, than the supple youngling she was. Stooping to retrieve her outgrown mantle—shabbier than ever but no longer despised—she shook the straws from it, huddled it around her again and kicked the rest of her scanty bedding into the corner. In the dimness she picked her way toward the door among the humped sleeping shapes, some stirring now, of the other Saxons, once free villagers of Hooë, Bexhill, Ashburnham, Wiltling, burgesses and cottars of Pevensey. There was Ulf the miller (but his mill was ashes), Almaer the smith's son (but the smith and smithy were no more), old Sidred the beekeeper (his bees all lost now along with their skeps and his house and his whole village), the widow Elveva who had owned her own fields, and Queneva the ale-wife, and pretty Marion who used to make the cheeses for Lady Edwina—now all hungry Norman drudges. Hooë, Bexhill, Ashburnham, Wiltling, Pevensey and God alone knew how many other villages lay in ruins, their inhabitants fled or forced into bondage like all these.

Forced into bondage like herself—thane's daughter no longer, as she had learned quickly and harshly. Her old life had vanished. Where now were her mother, Wulfric, Ragni, Nurse Editha, Lady Edwina and her daughters, even the little maid who used to comb her hair? Gone, like that other Juliana, the feckless child of eleven who had slipped away to run with the shore birds—and seen the striped ships looming from the mists.

The months since that morning had crept by like wounded things, dragging with them Christmastide, her own birthdate, the forty days of Lent, and an Easter that had brought no joy. It was spring now, still winter-cold though already past Whitsun, and she was twelve.

Quietly she let herself out into the morning. A cold wind swirled around her ankles and found every rip in her mantle. It brought the salty smell of the sea from beyond the palisade. Better by far than the hateful, sour-sweaty stench that clung about her captors, warriors and servants alike—the alien smell that had engulfed her in the moments before Jutta died. She knew it well now as the odor of harsh red wine and garlic; it was the smell of Normans—and still the smell of terror.

No Norman was abroad yet. The wide enclosure of the bailey was quiet except for stirrings in the cattle byre on the far side, the muffled thump of a stallion's hoof from the stables. She stood there, wondering where she could snatch the day's first bite of food, thinking for the hundredth time, *I must get away from them. I must. I'll go before nightfall.* Every day she vowed it. Every day she stayed on. There was no one to run to; no place to go. No food anywhere else.

The door behind her opened again. Queneva the ale-wife emerged with her old mother, both shivering in spite of the warm woollen headrails that hid their hair and were looped and draped around their necks and shoulders to hang to knee length.

"Springtime," said the old woman bitterly.

"It must warm soon," came Queneva's absent answer. She was looking warily toward the outer gatehouse, where the guard's face had appeared in the window; but he turned away indifferently, and she led her mother on, toward the laundering shed and their day's labor, with only one quick, sad glance at Juliana's feet as she went. For weeks, during the winter, she had stared and stared at them, seeming unable to look away, for Juliana wore her dead daughter's shoes.

21

But I am alive still, and I need them, Juliana told her silently. The daughter had died of the coughing sickness on St. Nicholas Day and Juliana had been sorry for Queneva, sorry for the girl. But she was glad of the soft ankle-high shoes as she crossed the trampled earth toward the well, for she had been captured barefoot.

She drew water, filled one of the earthen jugs that stood nearby, swung it to her head and walked on across the bailey. Passing through the inner palisade gate she stepped onto the drawbridge that led over the deep, encircling ditch to the high earthen mound on which the keep was built. There she paused, as always, to catch a glimpse toward the south of beach and sea meeting the gray, dim sky.

It was not her beloved beach at Pevensey—the beach of home. It was the shore at Hastings, in a patch of England made Norman long ago by royal gift to the Abbot of Fécamp. This drawbridge was part of the hated Norman fortress on which her Saxon friends and neighbors had labored, digging the slant-sided ditch ever deeper around both *motte* and bailey, and with the dirt they dug out piling the *motte* ever higher, after which the Normans raised their towerlike wooden keep atop the mound. At present the Norman Duke William—King William of England—was away in Normandy parading his triumph. He had left Wadard, the fortress commander, with only two score knights and archers and their retainers, to hold the Norman heel on Saxon necks. But two score were enough to keep their captives toiling while they themselves drank and caroused in their barracks—with this drawbridge prudently raised each night lest they be murdered in their beds.

The hollow note of the bell from Fécamp Abbey sounded prime. Time to deliver the shaving-water to the keep and lug back the pails of ordure that would be waiting there. Walking on across the bridge, Juliana glanced briefly to the left, toward the huddled thatches of Hastings, then quickly averted her eyes. She could never help looking, but she hated the sight of the village, despoiled and wasted, half-burnt, like Pevensey and every other Saxon place for miles around. Or nearly every other. Tiny Wartling, isolated on its marshy point, had escaped Norman notice. Wartling . . . the fortnight she had spent there, drifting like a ghost-maid about the marshes or sitting dazed in old Grim's hut, staring uncomprehending at Jutta's children, had been like some eerie nightmare from which she had been sure she would awake. But her attempts to leave had only ended in a worse reality—here.

If I had stayed in Wartling with Grim and those children, she reflected, I might be there still.

It was such a bitterly familiar thought that she did not realize, a few hours later as she stood plucking hens in the bailey's long workshed, that she had spoken the words aloud—until Rhonwen the bondsmaid answered them, at her elbow.

"Why did you leave, then? The more fool you, to chance it."

Juliana turned angrily. Rhonwen would never have spoken so, to a thane's daughter, before the world turned upside down. "How could I *not* chance it? I had to find where the battle was fought—what had happened to my father, and Sweyn, and King Harold and the earls his brothers. I *had* to go home to search for my mother and Ragni and Wulfric . . ."

So she had made two perilous venturings out of the salt marsh into the unrecognizable chaos that had been Sussex fields and towns. From her first sortie, into the great forest beyond the battlefield, she had come back, numb with shock and grief, but safe, to Wartling. From her second— to Pevensey—she had not.

"And did you find your mother, and Ragni, and Wulfric, all there in Pevensey and weeping for you?" came the flippant retort.

Juliana did not answer. What she had found, as Rhonwen well knew, was a mounted Norman knight rounding up a straggle of villagers—Rhonwen among them—like a herdsman bunching his sheep. He had glimpsed Juliana's pale Saxon hair as she tried to dodge out of sight, and spurring his big stallion straight toward her, effortlessly added her to his flock. The lot of them had ended up, stumbling with hunger and fatigue, ten miles away in Hastings—ten miles as the shore birds flew, thirty by the muddy foot-track they had followed around two harbors. Duke William had already moved his army and its rabble of priests and servants and attendants from Pevensey to Hastings, and begun to build this castle. Half a year later the captured Saxons who had finished it were still here, drudging slaves, with no homes left to go to, no fields to sow, no seed to sow in them, no oxen to pull the plows, no *witan* or even a folkmoot council to right their wrongs—not even an uncertain haven in a salt marsh.

Old Grim would have turned me out soon anyway, Juliana told herself. There was not enough to eat.

"*Zheely! Zheely!*" The Norman undercook was bellowing at her from the end of the drawbridge, giving a push to old Sidred the beekeeper, who was already starting across with his back bent under a load of brushwood. It was nearly *sext*, the undercook shouted in his pinch-nose Norman tongue; the cookfires would be ready in no time, and Normans did not like to wait for their meat. He turned back onto the bridge, bellowing at someone else, and Juliana relayed his message to Rhonwen and to Marion, who was gathering up the new-baked bread.

"How is it you know his tongue?" Marion asked her distrustfully, even as she divided a small damaged loaf among the three of them. Saxons snatched what food they could when they found a chance.

"I have a . . . I knew a Norman once. He made me learn some." It was a question Juliana was often asked, and she did not like to answer it.

But Rhonwen's dark eyes searched hers. "Do you know him still? As well to renew acquaintance—considering all." Her gesture took in their littered worktable, the gaunt Saxons around them, the whole alien bailey. As Juliana stared at her, she added impatiently, "He might shelter you. And your friends. If you were to ask it."

"Never!" snapped Juliana. "Never would I ask it."

"Is he so fearsome, then? A boggart?"

"Worse! A Norman!"

"So you said—else I would not suggest it!" Rhonwen retorted. "Small use would it be to ask aid of a Saxon!"

"I will not ask *him* for anything." She flung Rhonwen an angry glance, but seeing only incomprehension, lowered her voice. "He believed Duke William to be our rightful king! *He calls Harold Godwinson an oath-breaker!* I have heard him."

"Yeh-so?" Rhonwen gave a little shrug. "I have heard some in this castle say the same. Not only Normans."

"I, too," Marion murmured uneasily. "They say there was a banner Duke William carried into the battle—blessed and given him by the *pope in Rome.*"

"No doubt he stole it!" said Juliana.

"One could not steal such a thing!" Marion protested. "I do not like Normans either. But if they carried the pope's banner they had God on their side, and if *they* did, Harold Godwinson did *not,* and—"

"I will not listen!" Juliana burst out. "You know nothing! Nothing! My father Baldric fought scores of battles at Harold Godwinson's side! He died beside him! I will hear nothing against the Good King, the Ring-Giver . . ."

"Hsst!" Rhonwen warned, but too late. A heavy hand landed on the side of Juliana's head, knocking her half off her feet, making her ears ring.

"Silence! To the cookfires with these things!" commanded the baileymaster, shoving her basket toward her as he stalked away.

"Demon! Ox-turd!" Marion whispered. "Jilly—I meant only . . . I meant no . . ."

"Jilly, eat your bread before someone sees it," Rhonwen ordered. She pulled up the hood of the torn and stained man's mantle she had scavenged somewhere—Juliana did not care to think where or how. It was all she had to cover her thin rags. Then she shouldered the last haunch of the winter's dried meat. "Come along, both of you. The world is as it is."

Fighting back the tears of fury, Juliana stuffed half the chunk of stolen bread into her mouth, thrust the rest into her kirtle-front, and swung the heavy basket of plucked fowl to her head. *The world will not be as it is for long,* she was promising herself angrily. *Saxons will rise and make it again the way it should be—the way it always was.* Chewing hard, she started after Rhonwen. As she caught up she cast a sidewise glance at the dark slab of meat balanced across the bondmaid's shoulder, wondering bitterly if it had once been her own father's milk cow, or Wulfric's old Elf, or her mother Hildegund's gentle mare.

"It's mutton, Jilly," Rhonwen told her, half-mocking as always. "No need to grieve for it. What I'd like is a mouthful of it."

"Small chance you have of getting it," Marion put in.

"None! It's Norman fare. Not for the Welsh like me— or Saxons." Rhonwen's smile was tinged with malice. Like many another of her fellow Welsh she had grown up as a slave to Saxons, thanks to the capture of some long-ago kinsman in the endless border wars. The Welsh knew all about eating the leavings of foreign masters. Now the Saxons were learning, her smile said.

"I notice you're plump enough," Marion retorted as the three of them started across the bridge. "So could I be, if I chose to sleep in a dirty Norman's bed."

Rhonwen merely shrugged, and her shrug said she knew all about that, too. But as she glanced at Marion—widowed at sixteen by last autumn's battle, with a face like a flower—she added sharply, "You'd best keep well covered, my pretty ninny, or you'll get no choice! You, too, Jilly."

"I've nothing to cover with, save dirt," mumbled Juliana, who went bareheaded like any unmarried maid.

"Then mind you stay near me."

Marion obediently pulled the folds of her headrail down to her eyebrows and up to her cheekbones, and began to stoop and shuffle like Queneva's mother as she followed Rhonwen across the bridge. The transformation was surprising enough to make one stare.

Juliana marked it, but hung back, as the others passed through the inner gate, to steal another homesick look at the scrap of sea and beach and sky. Casting her usual unwilling glance the opposite way, down into the village, she glimpsed a scurrying small figure and paused a moment to watch, realizing that she had noticed the same child once before. He dodged among the huts, slipping behind one while a pig-drover passed, darting on to crouch behind a burnt-out cow byre, skirting an empty goose pen—always and again peering upwards toward the drawbridge. Or so it seemed, for she could see the ruddy oval of a face sometimes, instead of the round top of a head. It was a Saxon head, the hair ragged, straw-colored, tinged with red in the midday sun like a little, new-made thatch. He was venturing closer than before—much closer.

She peered with sudden painful attention, seized by the notion that there was something familiar in his darting, in the very shape of him—and especially in that worn woad-blue mantle with its wide band of once-white embroidery. She felt her heart give a great bound of surprise—of disbelief.

28

Surely it was Wulfric.

At that moment he halted again, staring up at her, then raised both hands, linked by their thumbs, and flapped palms and fingers like a bird's wings—and she was certain.

T H R E E

BEFORE SHE COULD MOVE THE BOY HAD DUCKED INTO A shed and she felt a heavy tread behind her on the bridge.

She whirled away from the Norman—it was the baileymaster, she knew his step—and hurried through the gate and across the flat top of the *motte* to the row of sheds that formed the kitchens. Turning her basket out on the trestle table, she began threading the hens on spits with hands made clumsy by their shaking, by a rush of wild, unreasoning joy.

Wulfric—not dead in the fire that had bloomed that day from the thatch of their father's Hall, but alive, and here, and flapping their old signal . . .

Unless it was his ghost. Or some cruel, light-headed fancy born of hunger—like those visions she sometimes had of Nurse Editha bringing her a huge honey-cake or a whole game pie. *Let this not be a fancy,* she prayed silently. *Or a ghost. Or a wicked changling brought by the Hidden Folk to look like Wulf and fool me . . . please, Holy Mary. Please, St. Juliana. Please, St. Agnes . . .* She did not know how to pray to the Hidden Folk or she would have done so.

The instant the last hen was spitted she snatched up her empty basket, along with one of the ale-jugs waiting to be filled. Avoiding Rhonwen's watchful eye, and before the undercook could think of a reason to shout, "Zheely!" she was back on the drawbridge, huddled against the gatehouse out of sight, and scanning the twisting Hastings alleyways.

Wulfric was nowhere to be seen. It was plain he was no longer there. Only a couple of the famished and masterless dogs, which were everywhere, wandered in and out of sight. She had no idea where he had gone—or indeed, where he had come from—or how to find him.

He will come back, she told herself. *He was here, I saw him. As God may strike me, I did not make it up.*

But as the wearisome day of fetching and carrying went on—so like every other—she grew less and less sure of that. Every time she crossed the drawbridge with her never-ending burdens she stopped to search for him again. It sickened her to think how many times he might have braved those dogs to come here, and she never seeing him. How was he living? Finding food? Saxons for miles around were homeless, landless, starving. She had seen them in the distance from the drawbridge, little roving, dangerous bands of them—and each midday they gathered in sullen knots outside the fortress gates, waiting for such scraps from the garrison's table as the captives had left them. Impossible that one small boy, only nine years old . . . *He must have found someone to look after him,* Juliana told herself. *Perhaps mother is alive after all, and he has come to rescue me . . .*

She was turning away, at mid-afternoon, when she caught a flash of movement almost directly below her, in the ditch itself. And there he was—hugging the *motte* slope to be out of sight of the inner gatehouse, waving wildly to get her attention. He was so close it took her breath. She cast a quick look over her shoulder, then fixed her gaze on him as he began signaling—palms pressed together and wriggling forward, like a fish swimming—and pointing toward the salt marshes west of Hastings. Then, with a gesture so urgent his whole small body seemed to plead—he beckoned her.

He was asking her to leave here—now, today—and meet him in the marshes.

Did he doubt me, she thought indignantly. He must know I would go to him *anywhere.* Into the marshes or into a bogle's den or headfirst into a well!

She nodded vigorously, signing to show she understood. Keeping an anxious watch on the gatehouse, she saw him scramble up the far side of the ditch and out of sight around the curve of the *motte.* Then swallowing hard, she turned away. There was no question that she would go.

But if he had come to rescue her, why would he plead?

It was easy enough to leave the fortress-castle, if you cared to risk the dangers outside. What was hard—impossible for the old or ill or very young—was getting back in again, if the sentries decided you were not worth feeding.

32

Normans rode out regularly—in mailed and well-armed groups—to help themselves to whatever they had overlooked before. But most Saxons inside the palisades where there was food took care to stay there.

To bring your brother back in with you was out of the question. Surely Wulfric must know that.

She had left the castle only twice, in early spring, with a mounted guard—both times sent by the garrison commander to find where the scurvy-grass grew on the edges of the village. His men were suffering the bleeding gums and blindness of the winter-borne illness, as were their Saxon slaves. Nobody had scurvy now. But the sentry might not think of that, Juliana reflected half an hour later as she moved nervously toward the outer gatehouse, carrying a small lidded basket she had picked up from the storage shed. No one had stopped her taking it—or seen her drop a double-handful of the horses' oats into it—or demanded where she was going. If need be she could bring back herbs of some sort, tell the sentry in his own hateful tongue that Wadard wanted them. Then he might let her back in. If need be.

Juliana shut her thoughts off. It was ill luck to hope for miracles.

Passing under the crude arch of the timbered gatehouse, she glanced quickly at the sentry. It was the one named Hugo—whom his fellows called "Mangebien," with good reason, for he could eat as much at one meal as captive Saxons could get their hands on in a fortnight. He was not ill-natured—for a Norman—though he had tried to wrest her mantle from her when he first saw it. It was the embroidered hem that had caught his fancy. Normans knew nothing of good raiment, she had decided after a winter of cleaning the mud from garments sewn of poor cloth, with clumsy trimming. By this time every knight wore a cloak of English wool, plundered from dead or living. Common archers like Hugo robbed their prisoners. To keep her own mantle through that freezing winter she had had to work patterns around the edge of Hugo's, using thread and needle he had seized from some poor Saxon woman, then watch him strutting like a peacock as he wore it.

He smirked down at her now, as she passed beneath the gatehouse window, and she gave an expressionless glance back. God alone knew when he would discover that she had embroidered pigs and snakes and trolls' heads into the twisting designs he wore.

Once across the outer drawbridge she turned away from the half-burnt village and hurried southwest, feeling exposed and vulnerable. The Normans had swept a circle of wasteland around the fortress; not a bush or tree or shed was left to provide cover, and there was no mounted guard behind her now. The hairs prickled on the back of her neck—and not only from the raw sea wind. But at last a dip in the sandy ground hid her, and a mile or so of rough and boggy going brought her into the marshes. It was hard, pushing through the reeds, and her shoes were soon soaked, but it was safe—from dogs and wandering Saxons if not from water-nixes—and if she knew Wulfric, he would have guessed the way she would come and be near, watching.

She was right. A low whistle—like a blackbird's—came

from somewhere, and she halted, returning the whistle and peering every which way, for sounds in the marsh deceived one. After a moment the reeds rustled and there he was, ruddy color and grin unchanged, though his voice broke as he gasped, "Jilly!" and hurled himself toward her.

"Wulfric—oh, Wulf . . ."

He was thinner, as she knew at once when she flung her arms around him, and far dirtier and shabbier than she had ever seen him. No doubt I am, too, she thought as they clung together, pushed away to examine each other, and then clung convulsively again, unable to say a word. It was hard to let go of him. She had not quite realized how she would feel—as if a wound had torn open, or a part of her mind jolted awake that had been asleep or numb. —

"I knew you'd come," he said at last.

"Wulfric, I was afraid for you—the dogs . . ." She tried to control her voice. "Wulf, I saw them fire our thatch, and I thought everyone was . . ." She swallowed again, hard. "Where have you come from? How did you find me? Is Mother with you? Is Ragni? Or Nurse?" She couldn't stop babbling, giving him no time to answer her questions, barely hearing his.

Finally they quieted themselves, found a tussock of dry ground among the reeds and mallow, and sat together on it, their hands still clutching and entwined.

"No one is with me," Wulfric told her. "I found you by asking. And watching. And hiding. And walking."

No one with him. I knew it, really, Juliana told herself. May God look after us. "You've been here all these months?"

"Only since St. Ambrose's Day."

Weeks ago. "But how do you get food?"

"I help Finn the Dane. He feeds me. Whatever we catch."

"Finn? That fisherman? Who used to—"

"The same. He lives nearby here, on the edge of the marsh. In some old fishing sculls—or under them. They'd never float, but they make a good enough shelter. If you have no other."

There was much he was not saying. His round blue eyes never left her face, searching it as if for something he was not sure of finding, and his abrupt, husky voice—it would be as deep as their father's when he grew to manhood—it held a question too. He had always talked in little bursts like this, watching for reaction. But no sudden mischievous sparkle lit his face now, and his old unworried composure had changed into something else. He looked older than his nine years.

No, he is ten now, Juliana reminded herself. He, too, had passed a birth date, three months back.

"Wulfric—where is Mother?"

His eyes wavered, then came back. "I don't know. Perhaps Winchester . . . if all went well."

"*Winchester?*" Juliana stared at him, but after the shock of surprise, her thoughts rearranged themselves and she did not know why she had not guessed it before. "Of course. She would go to Aunt Bergitta. And Uncle Robert. Even *now*," she added, with such resentment she could almost taste the gall.

"Why not now? He's our godfather."

"He's a *Norman.*" He was the Norman she had "once

known"—about whom she evaded Saxon questions—Robert fitzRobert, husband to her own mother's older sister.

"Then especially now," said Wulfric.

She turned on him indignantly. "You know our father never liked him. Or *any* Norman. Nor do I!"

Wulfric considered this. "Well, I don't like him either. He's always meddling. But he can't help where he was born."

Juliana made no answer. Old King Edward, who had spent his exiled youth in Normandy, favored Normans and had ever surrounded himself with them. Uncle Robert fitz-Robert, long an official in the royal court at Winchester, was a rich man and a worthy one. He had opened home and purse to his wife's young sister, Hildegund, when she was orphaned half-grown. Juliana knew her mother looked up to him as to some kindly god, not least because when she had yearned after a minor Saxon thane named Baldric instead of the Norman courtier chosen for her, her brother-in-law had silenced Aunt Bergitta's scolding and let her have her way. Indeed, he had become a zealous godfather to the children of the match. His godchildren themselves had found him overzealous—forever turning up on ceremonious visits, giving Hildegund tiresome advice about them which she always took. But this was irksome to no one but themselves. There was little real fault to find with Uncle Robert, Juliana was quite aware of this. Except that he was a Norman and called Harold Godwinson an oathbreaker, which she could never forgive.

"He quarreled with our father," she reminded Wulfric. "When Harold Godwinson became king."

"Our father is dead now," Wulfric said bleakly. "And a

Norman is king. Mother will be safe in Winchester . . . If ever she got there." He fell silent, but after a moment roused himself. "Perhaps, with all of them together . . . She took Ragni—and Nurse Editha and Lustwin, and one of the grooms. She nearly left it too late. They were firing the thatch as we ran. We kept waiting for *you*." His voice roughened. "Where were you? Not at your needlework in Lord Alfgar's hall! We sent a churl's boy running—"

"I—I slipped off to the shore. And then I couldn't get back . . ."

Gradually they fitted their stories together. Baldric had had a lookout watching from Beachy Head; word of the ships had reached him even as Juliana had stood staring at them on the windy shore. He had charged old Lustwin with the household's safety, sent riders to summon the scattered *fyrd*. Then he and Sweyn, with Lord Alfgar and his son Hereward and even Chelric—who was only a twelvemonth older than Juliana—had taken horse for London to warn King Harold Godwinson. It was the last Wulfric had seen of any of them, their five horses pounding into the distance on the Lewes road.

"But the King was not in London. Yeh-so. I know that now," he finished.

Everyone knew that now. On Michaelmas Eve Harold had been a week's march north, in York with nearly three thousand housecarls, fighting the Norwegians and his brother Tostig for his life and for England. Barely was the battle won when the news came of Norman ships in Pevensey. Harold and his battle-weary troops had spurred back to London, waited—though not long enough—for reinforcements to gather, and at dawn a fortnight later were standing shoulder to shoulder behind their wall of shields, facing William of Normandy's mounted knights.

"And did you know," said Juliana, "that our father stood at King Harold's side—next only to Earl Gyrth? All day he never budged from the lines, except to swing his ax. It was dusk when he was finally cut down. By then, there were no lines, and the King and both his brothers had fallen. Lord Alfgar fell, too. And Chelric in the first hour. Sweyn told me."

Wulfric stared at her, eyes wide. "*Sweyn* told you these things? Himself? You have *seen* Sweyn? He is living?"

"He was then. Two days after the battle. Wounded, and bloody, and . . ." Juliana searched for and could not find the words to tell how Sweyn had looked, there in the dimness of the great forest that spread out north of the battlefield, where she and other cautious searchers had found the Saxon survivors, lying among the trees or sitting silently, bathing each other's wounds with water from a little stream, trying to comprehend disaster. "An arrow had pierced his thigh—the left one. And there was a great gash in his cheek. They had put cobwebs on it to stop the blood, but there were not enough cobwebs. And I could not find comfrey or even waybread to ease his wounds."

"He will be scarred," Wulfric said. "He will look different."

"He looked different already, though not from the gash." Again Juliana searched for the words to make Wulfric see the white, strained face, the haunted eyes of their once light-hearted big brother. "I think he did not like to be alive when our father had fallen. And I think a battle was not as he always pictured it when he listened to our father's tales. As indeed, Wulfric, it is *not*," she added, feeling a shudder crawl up her spine as she remembered her one shocked, indelible glimpse of the battlefield on Caldbec Hill, strewn with scarlet rubbish that once had been men and horses, with stooped, slow figures of priests and women moving through it, searching for something recognizable to bury—and over all, the vast, resonant hum of thousands of flies. There had been nothing like that in the tales of glory that she, too, had listened to eagerly at Baldric's knee.

"But where is he now?" Wulfric insisted. "You have not told me where Sweyn went, what he meant to do!"

"I don't know . . . He said little to me, and made me go out of the forest and promise not to come back. But wherever he is, he means to kill Normans. He said the battle was not ended—and would never be ended while he drew breath."

They were silent a while. Around them the cat's-tail stems had begun to rustle and stir in the breeze of sunset. Juliana plucked one of the big, gray-green, hairy leaves from the nearest marsh mallow and stroked its velvet with fingers roughened and broken-nailed from her new life. The old life, with its fabrics soft as this leaf, its finespun wools, and the long mornings—half-tedious, half-absorbing —of work and chatter over the embroidery frames, had never seemed more distant.

There seemed to be nothing further to be said about Sweyn, who had turned his face from them. But there was much yet to learn about Wulfric. Juliana threw aside the leaf and her profitless thoughts.

"Why are *you* not in Winchester?" she demanded. "If you fled with mother and Ragni—"

"We fled no farther than Lewes, to the priory. It was crowded to bursting—folk from Pevensey and every hamlet around—babies, old ones . . . Saiwold the ironsmith brought his *goat*. But Brother Edric—that kinsman of Father's—"

"The monk with the lame arm. Yeh-so."

"He took us in. We only had three horses—Elf and the old bay, and mother's mare. And Elf was lame . . ." There was a spark of reproach in Wulfric's glance, which softened, as it met hers, into a half-smile. "Well, limping. We had to ride double. Mother kept saying we must hurry to Winchester, to keep Ragni safe, but then she would cry and say we must wait for you. Lustwin finally made her go on, next morning."

Juliana nodded, the picture clear and familiar. Unless their father—or Uncle Robert—was present, their mother always ended by doing as the servants advised. "But you?" she persisted.

Wulfric studied her with a slightly mulish look hardening his ruddy face. "I helped Lustwin make her go. I said I would stay at the priory—and wait until you came, and they could send for us. But once they left, I started back to Pevensey. I was *sure* I could find you. But . . ."

"You little fool!" cried Juliana. Her mind filled with pictures of the bloody market square, Normans swarming and shouting, hoofs clattering, Rhonwen screaming and the harvest-feast cow bawling as it was slaughtered. "You never *got* there?"

"I barely got back to the priory! Normans everywhere—

41

killing—burning barns—burning *seed corn*, Jilly." Wulfric's voice broke. "I found a fox's hole and squeezed in somehow and stayed till I could get back over the wall . . ." He managed a shaky laugh which Juliana could not join in. "After that, old Edric kept me under his thumb. I was there half the winter, fetching and carrying in the infirmary, scrubbing basins . . . But I finally got away—during Lent, it was. Climbed the wall behind the leper hut."

"Leaving Edric to tell Mother the Normans got you!"

"I doubt he'll need to." Wulfric studied his chapped hands, then met her eyes. "I doubt Mother got to Winchester. She never sent for me—all those weeks."

Juliana caught her breath. They *had* got there, they must have. They could not be lost, not now, just when she thought them safe—Mother, and Nurse, old Lustwin, little Ragni with her hay-gold curls . . . No. There were scores of reasons for delay—Normans on the roads, the winter mud, a lame horse. Doubtless they had all claimed shelter at some nun's minster, till travel was safer. "You did not wait long enough!" she scolded. "You should have stayed with Edric. Or started toward Winchester, not here!"

"But, Jilly, I got word of you! One day in Lewes I saw Oswig—that plowman of father's. Not much has changed for *him*," Wulfric added bitterly. "He lives in his same hut, he plows the same fields—but not for Father. For a red-nosed knight named Drogo, who holds *our* land, *our* woods, *our* sheep and horses . . . Aye, and some Norman count owns *him*, along with the whole of Pevensey and half of Sussex, everything that was Harold Godwinson's—"

"Stop—it's no use raging."

"They built a castle inside the old Roman fort. You can see it from everywhere—sticking up there, lording it over the town." Wulfric gave a savage kick to a clump of reeds. "Well, Oswig saw you captured, with some others—going toward Ashburnham, he thought. So I went there. Then I went on, other places, asking and asking. I knew you'd be somewhere, and I knew I'd find you. And I have."

"But why—how—" Juliana blinked the sudden tears back. "Wulfric, I can do nothing for you. Nothing! They would never let me bring you inside the palisades. You are better off with Finn the Dane."

"I don't want to go inside the palisades! Not to stay there, Jilly! You don't like it, do you? They make you work and work . . . And I don't want to stay with Finn the Dane."

"You want the ravens to feed us," Juliana said wearily.

"I want what I always wanted," Wulfric told her. "To go to school to the monks and become a scriptor, as Edgar promised me."

Juliana could only stare at him. That long-promised plan—like the rest of the world they had known before the ships came—seemed as remote as heaven. The famous school of Christ Church, their half-brother Edgar and his Benedictine brotherhood—they were in *Canterbury*. "Wulfric—we must get to Mother. Canterbury is miles and miles from here!"

"Closer than Winchester—by far."

"But in the opposite direction! And we don't know the way, and there's no food—"

"We can ask the way! We could not get to Winchester. Not now," said Wulfric, who was watching her closely.

43

"Norman warriors on every road west and northwest. Finn thinks there must be uprisings."

"May they prosper," Juliana said grimly.

"As for food, I can net fish! And steer a boat! Finn taught me . . ." Wulfric's voice trailed off. Even he, thought Juliana, could see that they had no net, no boat—and could use neither on a journey overland.

Yet they must live somehow—and they could not stay here.

She prodded her mind, forcing it into activity as she would kick a lazy horse. For seven months she had made no plan. Saxons were sure to avenge Harold, the scattered *fyrd* would reassemble, the uprisings would gather force and finally regain the land—she had never doubted it. Meanwhile, today was servitude, and tomorrow like today. Now, suddenly, tomorrow was blank as new linen. If they were not to sit here forever in these reeds she must make a new pattern—for her and Wulfric both.

The priory? Would accept a boy but not his sister.

Sweyn? Might be anywhere. Might be dead.

And Pevensey, for now, belonged to enemies.

They had never in their lives journeyed farther than Lewes. But they must go *somewhere*.

Winchester . . . *Uncle Robert,* she thought, and was swept by deep uneasiness. If one could be sure that Mother, and Nurse, and Ragni had truly reached there! If they had not . . . For an instant she stared straight at the possibility. Without Baldric, Hildegund, or even Nurse, Robert fitzRobert's authority over his godchildren would be absolute, his benevolent eye a hawk's, and they would be

44

truly conquered, she and Wulfric—they would grow up Norman.

She wrenched her mind from the picture. *Mother must be there. And I must believe it,* Juliana thought.

"We must go to Mother, Wulf. First to Pevensey—beg our bread from Oswig or one of our churls till it's safer to travel west . . ."

"It's safe *now* to travel east."

"It is safe nowhere!" She knew the whole Hastings area was Norman-infested. Exasperated, she waved a hand at a flight of ducks wheeling in over the harbor to settle among the reeds. "If we could fly like those birds—!"

"We can sail," announced Wulfric, surprising her. He saw it, and grinned. "Finn will take us out of Hastings in his boat, he has said so. Perhaps to Rye. We can walk after that. We'll find food somehow . . . Jilly, in a sennight— maybe two—I could be there, learning! Say you'll go!" As she gazed at him, out-argued, cornered, silenced, he added, "I'm going, I am. Alone if I must."

She believed him. Nobody was more obstinate. Or less realistic. And alone, in this week or two of his, between here and Canterbury, he could vanish—lost or starved, captured for a drudge or murdered for his clothes—she would never know. And she would never see him again. He was far more obstinate than she.

The voice of the vespers bell drifted over the distance from Fécamp Abbey. Juliana drew her skimpy mantle closer around her, and answered as she had always answered Wulfric. "I'll go," she said.

45

F O U R

WELL BEFORE PRIME NEXT MORNING THEY POLED THROUGH
the reedy shallows and set off around the edge of Bulver-
hythe harbor, safe in a thick mist that came and went eerily
among the greenish stalks close by. Wrapped in her mantle,
Juliana huddled in the boat's prow, straining to see around
her in the dim light. Wulfric was only a dark blur in the
stern beside the steering oar, half obscured by wisps of fog.
Clearer was the angular, changing shape of Finn the Dane
amidships, narrowing and shrinking as he bent forward over
the oars, looming and broadening as he slowly, powerfully
hauled them back. The only sound was the brief music of
dripping water when he lifted them, as if someone had run
a quiet hand over a harp's strings; but every stroke sent
the reeds alongside speeding backwards, made the boat
feel like a live thing, muscular as a fish. She found she was
breathing deeper, faster, gulping the salt-smelling air. It

was like galloping on Elf—like running with the shore birds on the beach. The whole journey began to seem possible.

We're escaping, she thought. *Wulf and I, we're getting free.*

Rhonwen's voice sounded briefly in her mind—a mixture of mockery, pity, and impatience—but she shut her ears to what it had to say.

The mist swirled higher overhead; the reeds thinned and receded. Soon they would be clear of the harbor mouth. "When will we raise the sail?" she asked softly.

"In good time," Finn rumbled, without looking around or breaking his even rhythm. He was an odd, solitary man, about whom she knew nothing save that he had always brought fish to Pevensey market. Dane he might be called, but his speech was that of the Hastings country, sprinkled with words and ways of saying them unheard in the rest of Sussex. Whatever he was, he had been a friend to Wulfric, and last night had given up his bedstraw to Juliana and slept in this boat. Baldric would have rewarded him. She would find a way to do so someday. He had made her remember that she was a thane's daughter.

There was a husky-voiced word from Wulfric, at the far end of the boat. Finn twisted his head to peer past Juliana at some land- or sea-mark among the swirls of fog, and nodded. After a moment his long, powerful strokes became short, battling ones as the boat suddenly heaved and struggled like a bird seeking to escape from a net. Juliana clung to its sides as it fought through the crosscurrents of the harbor mouth and slid at last into the swelling rhythms of the sea. Finn shipped his oars, reached to help Wulfric spread the crumpled sail, and together they transformed the little boat from a fish into a skimming bird.

By full daybreak of a fine blue day they were well out into the sea-lanes, with Hastings a smudge far behind and the coast a wavy, chalk-white band in the middle distance, now thin, now swelling thicker—like an embroidered hem on the mantle of the sea, thought Juliana, her fancy ballooning like the sail. The wheeling flights of shore birds might be worked in black thread just above, she mused, playing with the notion—and perhaps a pattern of reeds on the sleeve edges, with curling white swirls of mist.

Quickly she shifted her thoughts. Harking back was as foolish as hoping—more painful, and no use. Here in the sun and the fresh breeze, riding the boat's tilting dance, she could put aside past and future together until they beached in Rye.

By mid-morning they had sighted it, a steep dome of an island with a town on top, rising above the deeply indented coastline. Finn took the steering oar and sailed past the wide mouth of an estuary, rounded a point of land and entered Rye harbor, following a channel he plainly knew well. Once across the harbor and through the traffic of other fishing craft, he lowered the sail, and the little boat, shorn of its wings, crawled under oars to a mooring in a tiny cove well inland from the town, deserted except for a scull or two lying bottom-up among the marsh-grasses. Wulfric was out in an instant and steadying the boat.

As Juliana, clutching her basket, scrambled over the gunwale to join him, Finn pulled something from his tunic and

48

tossed it, with a faint smile—the first she had ever seen on his face. Wulfric caught the bundle, stared at it, and then grinned widely back. He stood waving as Finn, pushing off without further farewell, receded along with his little craft into the sunlit glitter of the harbor.

"Dried herrings—and a knife," Wulfric said. "We'll have *something* to start with."

We have the oats in my basket, Juliana thought, but decided not to mention them until the herrings were gone.

Wulfric, who had been squinting upward at the sun, then down at the shadows of the overturned sculls, turned away briskly, saying, "This way. Make haste." He started due north across the marshy flatland that stretched on three sides of them into empty distance.

Juliana followed with some misgivings. Plainly, he had learned much in his months with Finn and had been here before. But Finn was gone now, and the vast, lonely salt marsh all around made her uneasy. No saying what sort of creatures lived in those dank, secret tangles of bulrush and cotton-grass. Besides, she could see a high track, like a causeway, leading from the town's landgate away to the northeast. A woman with bundles and a pack-horse, an old man with a sheep, a salter pulling his two-wheeled cart, were trudging along it.

"We should be up there, where it is dry," she told Wulfric. "It would be safer."

"It would not," he said briefly.

At that moment, three horsemen emerged from the town's gate and cantered out along the highway. Wulfric's yank on her arm forced Juliana down among the reeds just

49

as the foot-travelers on the road scrambled off it, straight into the marsh, though the packhorse floundered, the woman fell, and the salter's cart overturned. The old man was not quick enough, and went down under the stallions' hooves. There was a flurry of action and frantic bleating; one of the horsemen turned back to the town, carrying the struggling sheep across his saddle. The other two galloped on, leaving the old man where he lay.

Juliana and Wulfric straightened from their crouch among the rushes and splashed on their way as fast as the treacherous footing allowed. Juliana, rubbing her cheek where one of the sharp-edged rush leaves had streaked it, said no more about the track and safety. Trolls and glaring-eyed bog-elves there might be, here among the frogs' houses. She preferred them to Normans.

It was the end of forgetting the past—and the future shrank to the next toiling step. The mud was cold and clutching; her feet grew numb, until she felt as if she were walking on mere stumps. The air reeked of rotting vegetation and the seabirds' fishy leavings. Ahead, Wulfric's woad-blue shoulders and tousled head receded steadily. The long fronds of the reeds rustled about them both like so many fragile swords, impossible to avoid, leaving tiny slices in the fabric of her sleeves and thin red cross-hatchings on all exposed skin. The only respite from the stinging were the patches of marsh mallow, which woke echoes of Nurse Editha's voice: *cold water only, to steep marsh mallow root—good for complaints of the chest, or a sickly child* . . . Pray God we will have no need of *simples!* she thought. But the tender mallow tops—silvery and furry as a moth's

wing—were also food. She gathered handfuls of the young-
est leaves into her basket as she slogged along. Far, far
above she could hear birdsong, and the occasional cry of a
gull. Here among the rushes there were only strange gur-
glings and slitherings, punctuated by an occasional sudden
loud splash that made her start uneasily. It seemed the
stumbling, squelching, eerie journey would never end.

At last it did; the reeds thinned into coarse, sparse grasses
and she could feel solid ground underfoot. She struggled
after Wulfric up a rough slope, and they both flung themselves down on the hard, warm earth.

After a moment Wulfric gasped hopefully, "Perhaps
there will be no more marshes."

Juliana did not answer. She was staring back over the
marsh, which stretched away far and wide, faintly glitter-
ing. From here she could see the tiny clouds of steam rising
from a score of scattered salt-pans. They made her think
of Grim, and Jutta's children, and Wartling—it seemed a
hundred years ago. In the distance the hump that was Rye
broke the flat horizon, and much nearer, to the east of
where they sat, she could see horses moving along the
causeway. Norman horses. With Normans astride them.

What am I doing here? she asked herself, with a sudden,
frightening sense of unreality. I belong with my mother.

Her own exultant thought of early morning—*We're escaping, we're getting free*—echoed in her mind, in Rhonwen's mocking voice. With difficulty she controlled her
panic. Had she thought to find Normans only in Hastings?
They were doubtless in every village, on every road. We
must avoid all roads, she warned herself.

But then, with sinking heart, she looked ahead, through the tangle of hazel and spindle tree and thickets to the dark wall of the forest behind it. "Must we go into the woods, Wulfric?"

Wulfric hauled himself up on his elbows, followed her glance, and shrugged. "Finn told me the shortest way across the marsh, then said to walk northeast. That's all I know of how to get to Canterbury."

And I know less, thought Juliana. Both of them stared toward the great forest of Andred—known simply as "the Weald." It lay full in their path, stretching east and west, she had no idea how far, like a great pelt covering the south of England. There was no way to walk northeast except straight into it.

Better that than Normans. "Come, then. If we must, we must."

They got to their feet and started—through the brushy border and into the tall trees. The sunshine grew patterned, then blotchy, then dimmed to a featureless twilight as the branches of oak and birch, beech and chestnut closed overhead, and the shadows that might have showed them "northeast" merged into gloom. Juliana pushed on, trying to keep her sense of direction as she dodged around the great fern-clumps, ducked under fallen trunks and skirted their vine-entangled stumps—aware that she might soon be wandering in circles in spite of everything. With every step her conviction grew that she should not be here, that all was wrong, wrong, wrong.

It was far too late for retreat. She found a meandering, barely discernible trail leading deep into the forest and kept to it, hoping human feet had made it, and for human purpose, though it had the look of an animal way. Certainly deer and foxes, wolves, perhaps bears and wild boars, had been here before them and would come this way again. So might the black-elves and giants who lurked in this dark home. She watched for them tensely, her skin prickling with gooseflesh, though she knew they could walk invisible if they chose. It was best not to think of it—if one could help it.

Wulfric was not thinking of it. Behind her, his voice came, cricket-cheerful, rasping across her stretched nerves: "Edgar told me I was born to be a scriptor. If I'm schooled at Canterbury—"

"Hsst! Do you want all Sussex to hear you?"

"—I might be a great one," Wulfric finished, though in a lower tone. "There is no one here," he added impatiently, and went on. "I might one day copy whole books and use colored inks and gold leaf. Edgar taught me a lot, you know. When he was a novice at Lewes."

"A pity you did not stay at Lewes—if you could be schooled there!"

"But I could not! Lewes has no school, it is a poor unlettered place, with no proper scriptors at all since Edgar was sent to Canterbury. They use *sheep* parchment! They have no vellum, no colored inks—scarce any books to speak of—"

Wulfric's scornful litany broke off as Juliana swept a hand over his mouth and pulled him behind a fallen tree-trunk. They crouched there, rigid, as a noisy scurrying somewhere to their left grew louder. Then Juliana breathed again as a

53

pig broke through the undergrowth onto the track, followed by several others. Wulfric grinned at her, but both kept silent, watching for the herdsman—until it occurred to them that there would be none, and should be no pigs, even, this time of year—only piglets, and those safe in some Saxon's sty. Grown pigs became bacon before Christmas, in normal times. But the times were not normal.

"They're wild ones," whispered Wulfric.

"Or tame ones gone wild," Juliana said, remembering the dogs rendered homeless by the burning and slaughter. These pigs did not look strong and hairy enough for wild ones—or tusky enough, either. She straightened cautiously. "We can go past them. But be careful of the boar."

"I could catch one!" Wulfric offered. "You drop a bean and they crowd around nose to nose to get it—and then you tie a straw rope to a hind leg—"

"Ninny! We have no bean, no straw rope—"

"But I have Finn's knife to butcher it!"

Juliana refrained from comment. Her first step out of cover scattered the pigs, which went squealing and snuffling into the underbrush and were soon out of hearing.

"Pity," remarked Wulfric as he followed her.

There was no use snapping at him, she told herself. Let him be cheerful if he could . . . Indeed, if they were truly moving northeast, he had reason to rejoice, since every step took him closer to his promised—his rightful—life. It *was* his rightful life, she knew that—designed for him, as he for it, perhaps by God's own pen. For him, northeast was the right direction.

But what about me? protested something within her. *No*

54

matter, she silenced it crossly. *God alone knows if we walk northeast or southwest anyway.*

The path had narrowed to a hand's width—scarcely that. It twisted and turned. Now and then the branches thinned far overhead, and Juliana searched anxiously for shadows which might point the way, but they leaned every way among the great mossy trunks. The forest went on and on, still and dim, inscrutable and endless as a dream-forest, until it seemed the two of them were the only humans in the world.

"Listen!" said Wulfric abruptly.

Both halted, Juliana with her heart pounding. But it was only water that he had heard—a faint musical burbling that spoke of a stream or spring somewhere near and made her realize she was parched. Eagerly they followed its voice and found it, a shallow brook running over its brown stones to form a secret, mossy pool, beside which they knelt and drank. Watercress, combed and stroked by the current, grew along its edges, providing a few mouthfuls of refreshing, if not filling, fare. Though she knew they would wilt soon, Juliana plucked some for the basket, longing vainly for one of her father's good leather water bags, or even a hog bladder like those used for lard. There might come a time when water would be a far worse need than food—but now they could take only as much as they could drink.

Reluctantly they left the brook to return to the little trail.

"Not that way." Wulfric objected. "Over here. We came past that big oak, I remember it."

"But here is a big oak. This is the one."

"No, truly. The trail is just yonder, I *know*, Jilly. We'll be lost if we go that way."

"We are lost already," she retorted, though she followed him. "We may find the trail, but who knows where the trail goes?"

"It must go somewhere," he said firmly.

However, they failed to find it. A weary, fruitless search later, they found the edge of the woods, instead. It was not the hazel thicket they had rested in that morning, but it was twin to it—and looking south, they could still see a great glassy stretch of marsh, with the sea beyond it. They had been wandering nearly due east. They might reach Dover this way, but never Canterbury.

They stood a moment in silence. Then Wulfric turned away abruptly.

"I'm hungry," he said in the blockish tones he always used to cover dismay. Walking over to a wayfaring tree— snowy with blossoms this time of year and a-hum with bees—he dropped down beside it and reached inside his tunic for Finn's herrings.

Juliana stopped him, grimly aware that there were times coming when they would need them worse. She, too, was dismayed; her whole body felt heavy with foreboding. But she was not surprised that they were far from where they had meant to be. "There is food here, Wulf. We have only to find it."

"We can find it tomorrow—when we do not have her-rings."

"We will *have* herrings tomorrow. If we find something else now." Scooping the wilted cress from her basket, she

56

put the herrings there instead, and tossed the herbs into his lap. "Begin on these."

He looked at them bleakly, then up at her. "Jilly? Will it take many days? To get there?"

"How should I know that, more than you?" Meeting his eyes, she sighed and added, "Forever, if we go through those woods. We must look for a road, Normans or not. And someone to ask. Come, help me find food."

Wulfric grumbled, but since fat hen and sweet cicely grew all around them, and a brief search yielded silverweed roots as well, he obeyed.

As they sat chewing their odd meal, which offered much chewing for small substance, he regained his usual good temper—in much the same way, Juliana reflected, that a cow grows ever more placid as it chews its cud. She did not know whether to be bitter or amused. *Perhaps I am only envious*, she thought.

"I mean to become a monk one day," he confided. "It is not a bad life—for a scriptor. *They* do not scrub basins. Until then I can sleep with the other pupils and eat in the frater-house . . . of course, you cannot," he added, momentarily troubled. Then his face cleared. "But Edgar is sure to look after you."

Juliana was silent, being sure of nothing about Edgar. Baldric's only child by Emma, the dead wife of his youth, Edgar was austere, assured, dark of eye and complexion, and nothing like their father. Juliana could feel no sense of kinship with him—or he with her, she suspected. But he had ever been Wulfric's idol—all because of his skills with a pen.

"We do not even know if Edgar is still in Canterbury," she said.

"We do, then. He came from there, when he last journeyed to see us."

"St. Swithin's Day! Much has happened since midsummer."

"Perhaps not to him," Wulfric pointed out. "Monks do not go into battle. And even Normans would not burn down a house of the Brotherhood!"

Juliana felt no such certainty—given a Saxon brotherhood—but she did not say so to Wulfric. She sat studying him as he chewed his root, his jaw mud-streaked and thinner, but obstinate as ever. She wondered what it would be like to be Wulfric—deeply sure of himself in spite of all, his mind steady on his dreamed-of future. He was ready to risk everything—had already done so—to gain it.

She herself felt that she was nobody, nothing, with no future she could picture at all. Once, before the striped ships came, she had been a thane's daughter—she had had a place. *"Good morning, Thane's Daughter!" "God's blessing, Thane's Daughter!"* folk had greeted her. Dimly she could remember—in that orderly life—knowing without thought that one day she would wed Chelric, that he would give her one pound of gold, thirty *hides* of plowland, twenty oxen, fifteen cows, ten fine mares, and six slaves, all to be her own forever, as their fathers had sworn it; that thereafter she would live in a Hall that would be hers and Chelric's, that she would direct the household, have children, teach the daughters to embroider. But Chelric was dead. Her father was dead. That other life had vanished—for

Wulfric, too—until God helped the Saxons to restore it.

Edgar alone was Wulfric's world, now that everything else was gone.

And what can be mine? she thought. I am not Thane's-Daughter now. I am not milkmaid—ale-wife—widow—weaver—cook. I do not know how to keep bees or even make bread. Until the Saxons rise what can I be—except the daughter of my mother?

A breeze, chill and dank, smelling of sea, swept in off the salt flats, making her pull her frayed mantle closer around her. The sun had hazed over.

Wulfric stood up, briskly swiping his palms together and then scrubbing them on his tunic. "Will we find the road now? And the 'someone' to ask our way?" he inquired.

"We will." She rose too, shook out her marsh-damp skirts, and picked up her basket. With a glance at the pale glow that was the sun, she turned her back on the sea and headed along the fringes of the woods, as near due north as the eastward-reaching arm of the Weald would allow. Northeast was Wulfric's direction, and his destiny—and she meant to get him to Canterbury, with or without God's help. But surely, for her, the way led west. Once she delivered Wulfric into Edgar's keeping, she would start for Winchester and her mother. Winchester—and Uncle Robert.

Again she felt the deep unease, the longing to be certain her mother was truly there, alive and safe.

I cannot be certain, she told herself. But go there I must, soon or late. There is no other place for me on earth.

F I V E

GRADUALLY THE HAZY AFTERNOON SKY DULLED TO GRAY
and the chill breeze turned raw and smelled of rain. When
the first spitting raindrops swept in from the south, Juliana
knew she must find shelter for the night. Already dusk was
gathering in the broken woodland through which they were
threading their way, and the forest proper loomed at their
left in a curtain of darkness.

They had found no trace of a road. They had seen no
one—not even from a distance, let alone close enough to
ask their way.

And Wulfric was limping, though he tried to hide it.

Juliana pulled him firmly into the half-shelter of a tangle
of bilberry, out of the wind, and said, "What ails your foot?"

"It's well enough, I can keep up," he protested, squirm-
ing, but when she merely kept hold of him and waited, he
met her eyes, his expression somewhere between chagrin

60

and tears. "It's not my foot," he burst out. "It's that knee I hurt Midsummer's Day when I fell off Elf, and it's going all swelled again and I *can't* lie abed this time and have comfrey poultices and valerian tea and Nurse to wait on me. But Jilly, it *hurts*, and what will we do if—"

"Hsst, be still. You're saying it's never plagued you till now—since Midsummer's?"

"It has," said Wulfric reluctantly. "The day I ran away from Lewes—but then I found Oswig's hut, and could leave off walking till it got better. And in Hastings once I stepped in a rabbit hole. But then Finn—"

"Yeh-so. Yeh-so." Juliana heaved a sigh and felt as if the last of her strength had drained away with the breath. Her feet felt heavy as stones. "We must both leave off walking for this day, I'm as weary as you." She glanced around, spotted a fairly dry nook behind a big moss-grown rock, and pointed. "Sit there while I find a sleeping place. By morning the swelling may be gone, and God willing, there might be comfrey growing hereabouts."

He hobbled obediently to the rock and eased himself down beside it, the ailing leg gingerly outstretched. His usually ruddy face looked pale and strained—but perhaps it was the light. Juliana put it out of her mind, and began—slowly, on her stone-heavy feet—to search for shelter.

She had to go into the edge of the forest to find it—a big rotting stump overgrown with lesser plants, its cavelike hollow half concealed behind bracken fronds. A pile of these, cut with Wulfric's knife, made a softer bed than the floor of the castle storeroom with its scanty straw, and as

Juliana helped Wulfric to it she reflected, again with that sense of unreality, that only two nights before she had slept in that storeroom, which now seemed half a lifetime away. In the twilit woodland she found a big patch of St. John's Wort—better even than comfrey—and made a poultice for Wulfric's knee, crushing the leaves to free the red juice, and binding it on as well as she could with a length of creeper.

"Now all we lack is supper," Wulfric said cheerfully, his spirits reviving. "And God be thanked, we have the herrings."

Finn be thanked, rather, thought Juliana. Or me, for making you eat herbs today instead. Aloud, she said only, "We also lack water. A pity God did not provide us with a brook just here—and a cup hanging from a branch. But if you want to eat dried fish and lie awake with thirst, I'll not stop you."

Wulfric looked thoughtful and presently remarked that he was not, after all, so very hungry. Juliana smiled and touched his ragged hair and judged it was time to serve forth her stolen horse-oats. A skimpy handful apiece kept them fully occupied for a while with trying not to break their teeth. By the time their emptiness eased they could barely see each other in the gloom. Huddled together for warmth, and too weary to fear trolls or wood-elves, they settled themselves to sleep.

Wulfric's wiry body soon went slack and his breathing grew deep and steady. But Juliana could not let go. The day's journey had tired her to exhaustion—as had every day's labor at Hastings. But at Hastings she had dropped down upon her straw at night knowing she had survived the day, that tomorrow would be no different, that she must survive that too—and never weep, never cringe, never suffer a word against Harold Godwinson, never cease hating Normans. It was all she asked of herself—all her father Baldric would have demanded. Indeed, it had seemed the utmost she could do.

Tonight that seemed to her a simple thing—merely to endure the old labors, defy the new blows, outwit the masters once again. Simple because all was known and expected and could be fought.

Now, all was unknown, tomorrow unpredictable, impossible to guard against—and *she* was master. There was no one to tell her what to do next or how to do it.

She tried to think how her father would manage—or Lord Alfgar—or Harold Godwinson—if they were lost in the Weald without food or friends, and Wulfric gone lame. But she could scarcely imagine them unarmed and afoot, let alone helpless or frightened.

She knew already what her mother Hildegund would do in extremity, for she had done it—and it was not to Juliana's liking.

Sweyn . . . ah, well, God-a-mercy, if Sweyn were here —were alive, and she could find him . . . Sweyn always knew what to do. He would work everything out, look after both of them . . .

But Sweyn was not here. Perhaps not alive.

Not even old Lustwin was here, though he was only a servant. Not even Nurse . . . Suddenly Juliana longed for Nurse with a desperation that brought the remembered sharp scent of dried herbs and aniseed, the very sound of a voice always brisk, always sure.

Trying in vain to visualize Nurse Editha curled in this hollow stump, Juliana slept at last.

The next day God smiled. They awoke to a clearing sky, found a mug's measure of rain collected in the hollows of the big rock, and Wulfric's knee mended.

"You must take care, nonetheless," Juliana told him as they gathered a leafy breakfast. "It will likely go lame again when you tire. None of your bouncing and jumping. Walk like a monk to his prayers."

"I will, then!" vowed Wulfric.

Now if only I knew how to find a road, Juliana added to herself as they set out doggedly northeast, through a spinney of birch and oak as trackless as all the others, which soon merged into dense forest. Once more, the Weald enfolded them.

But God was still smiling. Within an hour they came quite suddenly upon a clearing, at the far side of which stood a small hut. It was partially sunk in the ground, so that its thatch, steep-pitched, with a thread of blue smoke curling upward from the smokehole, rose directly from the forest floor. They halted warily, noting the tiny garden, a pen in which a few hens pecked, a tethered ewe. Beyond the hut stood a little wattled building with a crude cross of sticks nailed up beside its doorless entrance. As they peered at it, the figure of an old man appeared in the opening.

All was instantly explained. He was shabby and barefoot—but also shaven, clipped and tonsured, plainly by his own inexpert hand.

"A holy man," whispered Wulfric. He got to his knees

—awkwardly, as he remembered to favor the left one—
and Juliana did also, crossing herself and praying the hermit
was not so holy that he would drive them at once from his
refuge without allowing a word to be spoken. She need not
have worried. He raised his hand in blessing, then stooped
out of the low doorway and hobbled toward them, smiling,
blinking happily, and already asking questions.

In a soft, wavering voice that sounded rusty from disuse,
he asked if they were hungry, if they had lost their way,
where they had come from and where they were going,
what their names were. Before they could answer he asked
straight on—if they liked milk, and how often they said
their prayers each day, and when they had left home. Meanwhile he was hovering around them like a shepherd with
two strays, urging them by little gestures and nods toward
his hut, beckoning them to a seat on the flattened log which
lay alongside his door. And when he finally fell silent and
they burst into a jumble of eager speech, they discovered
that he was stone-deaf and all replies must be made somehow by sign and mummery.

Juliana's soaring hopes tumbled into dismay. "But how
will we ever ask the way to Canterbury?" she whispered.

"No matter," Wulfric muttered. "I will find *some* way to
tell him that I like milk and am hungry enough to eat the
ewe herself." He launched at once into a performance that
needed only a harpist to be worthy of a thane's banqueting.
The hermit, who called himself Brother Saiwold, showed
every sign of delight and none of insisting on more difficult
answers. He was soon ducking into his dark little hut again,
emerging with a bowl of gruel and one of stewed nettles,
beckoning Wulfric into his garden to pull a few onions while

65

he milked the ewe into his only mug. He had only one spoon, also, carved of horn, but his guests found that no obstacle to sharing the most bountiful meal either had had in months.

Afterwards, he asked again where they were going. Juliana mouthed "Canterbury" as plainly as she could, mimed a tonsure, a monk on his knees at his devotions, and another pulling on a bell-rope, then pointed in the direction she hoped was northeast.

To her relief the hermit's face lighted. He repeated, "Canterbury. It was my home among men. The dean is an old friend—since we were boys like you." The old man grinned and nodded at Wulfric. "His name is Henry. Give him greetings from Brother Saiwold if you see him." Thoughtfully he added, "He does not approve his arch-bishop—Stigand. Nor do I! A man excommunicated by five popes! Ah, well. God will send another in His good time. Now, my children." He raised a gnarled finger and pointed—not where Juliana had pointed, but at near right-angles to it. "You must walk that way until you see a track, then follow it to your left, mind, not to your right. By the hour of nones, you will come to Benenden. There are kindly folk there, and they will show you the old stone road. That road will lead you through the Weald." He smiled and raised his hand in blessing. "God go with you. Give my brother-kiss to Henry. Though not to the archbishop. No, not to Stigand . . ." Shaking his head severely, he turned, still muttering to himself, and hobbled back toward his little oratory, no doubt to make the next of his ceaseless devotions.

"God go with *him,* too," murmured Wulfric gratefully.

"And be thanked for leading us to him!" said Juliana with her whole heart. "And protect him from Normans!"

"God would not lead any Normans here," Wulfric declared as they started in the direction the hermit had pointed.

"At least He has not—so far." She pondered that, uneasily. "I think Brother Saiwold did not even know about the ships. About the battle. Did it seem so to you?"

Wulfric considered, and shrugged. "It may be."

It may be, thought Juliana, that he does not even know Harold Godwinson is not our king, but lies moldering, none knows where—hacked to pieces, Sweyn said, and the pieces scattered . . .

"As well for him if he does not know," Wulfric decided.

Juliana murmured, "Yeh-so," but she could not help wondering how long it might have been since Brother Saiwold had been to that village of Benenden, and seen with his own eyes those "kindly folk." Resolutely she turned her thoughts, and a few moments later Wulfric announced, "There is the track!"

It was a plainer track than yesterday's thread of a path that had meandered and twisted and vanished. This one showed signs of enough use to keep it visible among the ferns that lapped the tree trunks like a dark green sea—a sea increasingly rolling, as the ground under their feet tilted into ever more hilly terrain. They followed the trail some hours, stopping sometimes to rest Wulfric's knee and once beside a spring to drink and eat the watercress.

Gradually Juliana felt her tensions easing, the despairs

of last night fading, confidence cautiously rising. Here, the world seemed much as it had always been—though near-empty of people. They saw no one except a charcoal-burner, tending his smoky fire a furlong away across an open patch, and an old man in a hooded tunic who appeared far ahead of them on the track, hobbled along busily for a little time, then disappeared down some hidden way as abruptly as he had come. Of the Weald's native dwellers they only caught glimpses—the flick of a squirrel-tail, a flash of white underwing—though the forest reverberated with the incessant twitter and flutter and rustle of their presence.

In the late afternoon they crossed a once-cultivated field, now weedy and idle, and from the crest of the little rise beyond it, saw the first house of Benenden. It was a black-ened skeleton, forlorn amid its ashes.

The peace of the long, unthreatening day was shattered in an instant. The flesh crawled on Juliana's arms and scalp as she stared at the familiar, ugly face of ruin. Plainly, the Normans had been here, leaving Benenden as they had left Bexhill and Wilting and Ashburnham and Guestling—and Pevensey.

She glanced at Wulfric's bleak profile, tried to speak, and could not.

"Yeh-so," he muttered. After a moment he stirred. "Will we go down anyway?" he asked.

"We will, certainly. But take care."

Cautiously they picked their way down the last slope, staying within the shelter of the trees until they could see beyond the first burned house into the little rutted street.

It was a short street, set with no more than a dozen houses, with a savagely demolished Hall and its outbuildings at one end, an untouched church at the other.

As they stood peering at the sturdy little stone church, a woman came out of its round-arched door lugging a large basket, crossed the churchyard, and began spreading laundered garments on the low wall and the nearest gravestones.

"She is living there!" Wulfric whispered.

It was such a homely, common action, despite the oddity of drying the washing in a churchyard, that both of them started forward, their caution forgotten. The woman's was not. She heard them, whirled, picked up a fist-sized stone, and let it fly.

Wulfric seized Juliana's hand and yanked her, stumbling, toward the trees, but the woman cried, "Halt!" and Juliana twisted free. "We are children," she told the woman in a voice shaky with alarm. "We are Saxons! Can you not see that?"

The woman had already raised another stone. She did not drop it. "Come closer, then."

"It's what we *were* doing," Wulfric muttered, rubbing gingerly at his knee.

When they stood an arm's length from her in the churchyard, she said, "Yeh-so. You are children," and dropped the stone. "What do you want, then?"

"The hermit sent us here. To ask our way," said Juliana. She could not blame the woman, but was frightened by the way she continued to stare at them, narrow-eyed, head and lower lip both outthrust.

"He said," Wulfric added belligerently, "this place was full of *kindly folk* who would help us."

After a moment the woman's expression altered slightly; her face seemed to change from stone to wood. "And so it was, once." Her squinting glance swept down the street of ruined houses and up toward the weed-grown field they had crossed, then came back to Juliana, who now realized that she was nearly blind. "Hermit, you say? Brother Saiwold lives yet? They did not find him?"

There was no doubt whom she meant by "they," and Juliana reassured her. The hermit's name seemed a talisman to the woman. Her face softened further, from wood to aging flesh. She took them into the little porticus—a tiny chamber built onto the side of the little church—and gave them a mug of water, and a morsel of bread for Juliana's basket, and finally pointed along the weed-grown stone road in the direction of Canterbury. It was an ancient road, which did not curve or seek the easiest way, as men and horses naturally walk, but cut straight across everything after the Roman custom, tidy as if a line had been ruled—save for the gaps where some of its great, squared stones had been dug up by folk to build with.

"Take care. There are thieves," the woman warned as they set out. They hesitated, startled, but she added nothing, only shuffled back to her interrupted laundry, leaving them to make of it what they could.

"We have nothing to steal," Wulfric commented with a shrug as they went on.

He was mistaken, as they discovered late in the afternoon, when their shadows stretched long in front of them and they had dropped down wearily by a roadside spring to eat Wulfric's herrings at last. Juliana had barely opened the basket when she heard a rustle among the spindle-trees behind her and a voice said, "I'll have that, little maid," and the basket was plucked from her hands.

"*And* the mantles," said a deeper voice. "Both of them. Haste, boy. Up with you!"

Wulfric, who had sat stunned and gaping, was suddenly yanked to his feet and stripped of his mantle by a stocky gray-haired man with flowing mustaches and a ragged tunic. At the last moment he came to life with a yell, clamped both hands to his property and clung so fiercely that he was swung off his feet, still clinging, only to be flung aside. He lay gasping and clutching his knee as Juliana, still beating off the younger man, felt her elbows pinned from behind by hands as iron-strong as her father's. It was folly to struggle against a grip like that, as she had learned early and well. The young thief peeled her mantle off unceremoniously over her head as his comrade held her.

"Shame, you cowards! Child robbers!" she choked as she shook her hair back, half-strangled and hot with fury. "Saxons both, and robbing other Saxons! We are *thane's* children! My brother is fighting Normans, he is so! If he were here now he would fight *you*, swine's kin, slave's slaves—!"

She spat with all the force she could summon at their retreating backs, then dropped down beside Wulfric as the tears came, stinging her eyes and knotting her throat. "Oh, Wulf, if I had but let you eat your herrings yesterday!"

"They'd be gone by now anyway," Wulfric muttered. He was still nursing his knee, staring at the thicket into which the two men had vanished.

"Gone, yeh-so! But not inside those great, ugly . . . May

71

God strike them both as they take the first bite! . . . Are you hurt, then?"

"My knee only. Jilly—did you think you knew that man? The young one? With the funny ears."

"*Know* him? What are you saying?"

"I thought I had seen those ears somewhere."

"In your nightmares," retorted Juliana. She had been too frightened to notice ears—or years—only the Baldric-like strength of hands that had brought homesickness and bitter longing sweeping through her even as it quashed her struggle. Oh, if Father were here! she kept thinking. He would batter their heads together, he would slay them with one blow . . . "Now we have nothing to eat, or to wrap ourselves in for sleeping. God's mercy they did not want my kirtle, or your shoes!"

"They may come back. They forgot my knife." Wulfric remarked. He stood up, sighing, and took a few cautious steps. "I can go farther. A little."

Juliana, weary of foot and heartsore to find Saxons could be pitiless as Normans, felt she could not—but knew she must. They dragged their way up the next hill and over its crest, and found another cobwebby hollow stump among the taller trees, well away from the road. With a pile of bracken-fronds to line it, neither hunger nor the evening chill kept Wulfric long from exhausted sleep.

Huddled against him as much for consolation as for warmth, Juliana soon slept too—and dreamed of the striped ships for the first time since leaving Hastings. The old terror ran its familiar course, and though she knew even in her dream that she was dreaming, it was no less terrible. At last, still straining to cry, *"Father! Normans! Father!"* she awoke, clammy with cold sweat, thinking she had heard a voice from somewhere in the silent wood, quietly calling her name. She lay rigid, disbelieving. After a moment a nightbird whistled—a muted, two-toned note—another answered indistinctly. Birds, only. Yet she listened, wary of thieves and signals.

The bird called again—bird, or man. She should make sure, certainly. Beside her, Wulfric came to life and struggled to sit up; Juliana shushed him and crawled from their ferny bed. Something about the still darkness told her they could have slept little more than an hour.

Again the whistle came—from the direction of the road —and she crept toward it. As the trees thinned into broken woodland she saw them, two figures picked out by the waning moon, walking slowly along the wood's edge, peering and whistling. One was the younger of the two men who had robbed them. But the other was not the stocky older man with the iron-strong hands.

The other was Sweyn.

With a cry she stumbled forward over the uneven ground and flung herself into his arms.

S I X

"*SWEYN* ROBBED US?" SAID WULFRIC—HIS VOICE THIN, as if he were trying to believe it.

"He did not, then! What are you saying? Are we not wearing our mantles again? Are we not eating his food?"

"They ate my herrings."

"Not Sweyn! Those others. Last night before they fetched Sweyn, even. Sweyn knew nothing about it!"

"Beorc knew. He *took* them from you. And he knew *us,* all the time. And I, him. I remembered those funny ears."

"Well-so, he knew us," muttered Juliana reluctantly. And robbed us anyway, he and that other, her thoughts went on, appalled. And Sweyn is of their company, and they of his . . . Is it a company of robbers, then? Sweyn went to fight Normans—not Saxon friends. "It may be they cannot find food enough. They cannot fight Normans if they starve."

"What good to starve Saxons while they do it?"

"No doubt they take from Normans when they can. They did not know it was all we had."

"Oh, did they not, then? I'll wager they thought our baggage-carts were just ahead. Or just behind, following with our servants!"

Wulfric's judgment was implacable. And indeed, it was hard to defend Sweyn's companions—and therefore, Sweyn. They do what they must, she argued with herself. I cannot know their hardships or I would understand . . . "They are not the first warriors to live off the land," she said, to end the subject. "And had Beorc not known us and shown Sweyn our mantles, we would not be here now."

Wulfric chewed on his hearth-bread and did not answer, but stared around woodenly at the rebels' camp. Juliana suspected he would have preferred *not* to be here now— that he would rather be walking on toward Canterbury, with his mantle or without. He had greeted Sweyn last night with a boisterous elation, unclouded as her own, but it had dimmed when he saw at Sweyn's side the young robber who had snatched Juliana's basket—Beorc, the carpenter's son, from Pevensey—and grasped that the two were allies, equals, rebel comrades-in-arms. He had stood mute while Juliana poured out their story to Sweyn, but when Sweyn decided they must come with him, he had got his stubborn look and drawn back.

"How far, then? My knee is ailing. And this is our road."

Astonished, Juliana swept his objections aside. Never mind the knee, Sweyn and Beorc had ponies, tethered back in the thicket near the spring. They could always come back to the road—in a day or two, a week—if Sweyn thought it best. Buoyant with joy herself, she could not imagine why he would not wish to go with Sweyn—anywhere, any time, without question. To be with Sweyn was to have kindred again, to find a piece of the old life's pattern, regardless of how it had happened. How could he not see that?

Warned to keep silence, and riding double—Wulfric behind Sweyn because he would not go near Beorc—they had followed a moon-dappled track an hour or so through thick forest in which it seemed nothing but nightingales lived. Both were sagging with fatigue against their guardians' backs before they saw the glimmer of firelight and figures moving against it. The beds they shortly tumbled into were little different from the one they had left in the hollow stump, but their own mantles were thrown over them, and Sweyn was near. Juliana slept without dreaming.

Now, in the pale, pearly light of morning—a light like the inside of a shell, she thought—she sat with Wulfric on a bank amid the wild strawberry, and ate the rebels' rough bread and looked down upon the camp, nearly a score of makeshift shelters scattered over a sloping hollow and into the forest around it. An iron-smelter had once had his forge here; the slope was pocked with his diggings, and his crumbling bloomery-hearth leaned into the hillside. A swift creek prattled nearby. In the clearing, three cookfires sent up transparent gray ribbons. A few men squatted on their heels around the nearest; women tended the others, moving about with jugs and iron pots. Juliana saw one or two small children fetching twigs and sticks to feed the flames.

"You see, there are families here!" she told Wulfric. "It is like a village. People have their kin around them, and their duties, and . . ."

"It is not like a village. Who is thane?"

Juliana's chin went up a trifle. "Why should it not be Sweyn? He is a thane's son."

"And comrade to a carpenter's. I think there is no thane. Only, it may be, some captains. It is like a *fyrd*."

"Yeh-so!" The idea appealed to her fiercely. "A *fyrd* gathered to fight Normans—to take our land back! Wulfric, we will stay and help them! We could fight too—or we could tend fires or ponies. Canterbury can wait until—"

"Canterbury will not wait!" Wulfric scrambled to his feet, glowered down at her. "*I* will not wait. You promised. I hold you to it."

She glowered back at him for a moment, then saw the panic behind his glare. "We will go," she told him. "As God hears me, Wulfric, I will get you there!" *But I will come back,* she vowed silently. *There is a place for me here. I could help Sweyn. I could be more than just the daughter of my mother.*

"I want to go soon," Wulfric said. He was limping restlessly about, kicking at the strawberry blossoms, fidgeting with the long thorn that fastened his mantle on his shoulder. His old carved bone pin was long gone—traded for food during his wanderings toward Hastings, Juliana supposed —as gone as her silver one, which Hugo Mangebien the Norman now sported upon his snake-and-troll embroidered mantle. *And may it stab him through, one day,* she thought.

To Wulfric, she said, "We will go when your knee is

rested. When we know the way. I will ask Sweyn when he comes."

"If ever he comes," Wulfric muttered, but he dropped down beside her again and stretched the knee out.

Both of them looked beyond the cookfires to the two big birches that marked the way to the forest trail they had ridden last night. An hour ago, before they were well awake, Sweyn had leaned over them with bread and a promise to return, then hurried across the clearing where two men waited with ponies. He had not come back. But even as Wulfric spoke, a man appeared between the trees leading a horse, followed by another and another. Two of the animals carried not men but deer carcasses, slung over the saddles with the feet tied beneath. The third carried Sweyn. He dismounted, looped his reins over a branch while his eyes sought and found Juliana, who had leaped up to wave, and a moment later he was climbing the slope toward them.

He was gaunt, unsmiling, older and harder than the Sweyn in her memory. The gash of battle on his cheek had healed to a livid scar that pulled slightly at the outer left corners of eye and mouth. In the glimmer of the moon last night Juliana had scarcely noticed it; this morning she could see nothing else. It changed his expression—he did not look like Sweyn, though he was tall and fair as ever.

But he is Sweyn, she told herself, feeling relief swell like a great bubble inside her. He came to find us last night, he made them give back our mantles, he took care of us. He is my brother. Nothing can change that.

"So," he said abruptly. He dropped down on the bank beside them, his white-blond eyebrows puckered. "Now we must talk. You have found me. How?" As they stared at him blankly, he added, with some impatience, "Who told you where I was? How to come to this camp?"

"No one told us," said Juliana.

"We were not looking for you, only the way to Canterbury!" Wulfric told him. "Jilly said so last night—had you but listened."

Sweyn blinked, then his frown cleared. "Canterbury. I remember. Good. Now, attend me. This camp must stay secret. You must tell no one—no one. You must swear to me. Once you leave here—"

"What need to swear?" said Wulfric. "I daresay we could not tell the way if we would—I could not even find the Roman road again, or that spring, or—"

"We will say nothing to anyone, *I* swear it!" Juliana cut in. "I vow by our kinship, by Father's sword, by the word of Harold Godwinson—"

Sweyn threw her a glance that was like a dash of cold water, startling her silent. "Rather vow on your own word, Jilly," he told her. "I will trust that."

She thought she had misheard what he was saying—what he seemed to be saying. "How so?" she faltered. "Always we used to swear on Father's sword and Earl Harold's word—all my life I've done so."

"And I, and I. But no life is as it used to be." He silenced the questions crowding to her lips with a smile and a wave of his hand. "I mean only that you are a trusty maid and I believe you. Wulf, also." His clear gray gaze switched to Wulfric. "We fight for *all* Saxons here. All English. The camp must not be betrayed."

"I will betray no one," Wulfric muttered. He pulled at

the grass-blades under his elbow, tossed them away, and sat up. "How do you fight, then, when there is no battle? By robbing Saxons of their herrings?"

"Wulf," protested Juliana, but Sweyn answered, grimly and in full.

"We pick off Normans one by one, little brother—as we would pick off rats from the grain-stores or ravens from a corpse. We watch the roads they ride and the alleys they walk. We have an arrow for every Norman heart. Do you understand me? We mean to rid this land of them—so England may have an English king." He paused, looking from one to the other of them, then went on in the same even tones. "Meanwhile, we must eat. Saxon herrings, if need be. As for your mantles—" he glanced absently toward the cookfires where the women and children clustered "—they were needed. But you have them back."

Neither was thinking of mantles now. "Do they never catch you?" asked Wulfric in subdued, scared tones. "Do they not chase you on those great horses, spear you, kill you—?"

"Wulf, men fall in any battle. We've lost many—but fewer of late. When Normans find a dead man nowadays they do not find us."

Juliana's skin crawled as she remembered blackened ruins, Norman vengeance. "Do they not find—someone? Who may be innocent?"

"Certainly. They ravage the nearest village and all in it —unless the body is proved English. A dead Englishman they scarcely heed." Sweyn's scar dragged at his eye as a faint smile twisted down the corner of his mouth. "So we take care to make our raven look English before we leave him. The villagers will swear to a man it is poor Almaer the churl who lies there—kin to most, known to all."

Juliana thought of blond Saxon hair, flowing Saxon mustaches—and the shaven-faced, shaven-naped Normans. "But how to make Norman look Saxon—?"

Sweyn said briefly, "It can be done," and began to question Wulfric about their mother.

The image of the grisly, flesh-strewn battlefield at Caldbec Hill rose like a specter in Juliana's mind, and she was glad he had not described his methods. It was a strange, bloody life her Sweyn was living—even for a warrior-thane—for it was all war and *fyrd*-service, never any coming home to Hall and spring plowing and kin. His battles did not sound like any she had ever heard her father tell of. But he was fighting Normans, all the same.

"I want to help you!" she burst out. "I do not wish to go to Winchester and Uncle Robert, I could stay here, mend your clothes, it may be—"

"What are you saying?" Sweyn turned, frowning. "In God's name you must not go near Uncle Robert, you must have nothing to do with any Norman! Do you understand that, Jilly?"

"I do, certainly . . . But our mother—"

"Our mother is—our mother. And had no choice. But you must not put yourself in Norman hands. As to Wulfric—Christ Church Priory is a good place for him. In the cloister with his ink and pens. You must take him to Canterbury, to Edgar."

81

"I am taking him to Canterbury, am I not? But it is *my* choice to come back, then—live here with you—"

"Here? Little ninny, you cannot live here—a maid, my *sister*—with all these men!"

Juliana gaped at him, gestured toward the cookfires. "How not? There are many sisters here, and wives and children—kinswomen—"

Sweyn frowned blankly for a moment, and followed her gaze as if the sight below were entirely new to him. Then he came near looking like the old Sweyn, her teasing brother. "No doubt they are kin to some men, but not to ours, Jilly. They are only . . . women who follow warrior camps. Wantons and their brats."

Wantons only. Yet there were two score rebels or more in this camp—young men, old . . .

"Then where . . . are their sisters—and wives and children?"

His voice somber again, Sweyn said, "God knows." After a moment his glance focused on her, sharp and thoughtful. "You should not go upon the roads alone—a young maid with no protection."

"She is not alone, then!" Wulfric said indignantly.

"Wulfric has a knife," added Juliana, defensive herself after being made to feel a foolish child, mistaking those women for family-kin. "Anyway the only road we have found so far was empty."

"Except for thieves," muttered Wulfric.

"The roads between here and Canterbury will not be empty," Sweyn informed them. "Half the world is trying to go somewhere else. There'll be thieves in plenty—wolves on two legs—Normans. Stand up, Jilly . . . both of you. Yeh-so," he murmured. "Alongside Wulf you are tall as a woman grown, or near enough." He got to his feet himself, said, "Wait here," and strode off down the slope toward the women's cookfires.

They gazed after him. It was a moment before either spoke. "It's plain he thinks me a poor creature," Wulfric said in a voice as bleak as Juliana's thoughts.

"Not so, Wulf—he only said—"

"Runt of the litter, fit only for pens and ink, which *he* thinks worthless. Well, I can bend a bow—and hit a hare running! But I don't care to. *He* cares for nothing but spilling blood."

"The blood of Normans!"

"Yeh-so. His ravens! Well, who's to stop three more coming from Normandy for every one he kills?"

The same thought had crossed Juliana's mind, to be pushed hastily into the background. Wulfric's blunt logic dragged it back. It seemed small use to pick a few Normans off the roads when hundreds lived in Saxon Halls and owned vast sweeps of Saxon fields, along with the beasts and plowmen—Oswig and the others—owned whole towns, like Pevensey, and the townsmen. Could rebel arrows change all that?

"I—don't know," Juliana faltered. "But he must fight—a proud warrior like Sweyn, a thane's son . . . That is—you are thane's son too, Wulf—"

"I am, surely. Without an ell of land to inherit. And Father's dead." Wulfric had his blockish look. "I will keep to my pens and ink, so I will. And live my life. But Sweyn won't, Jilly. He's throwing his away."

"He is fighting," insisted Juliana miserably.

What can he do else? she was thinking. No life—just now—was as it used to be. But surely some things did not change—even death could not change them. Why should she not swear still on her father's sword, on Earl Harold's word? The question haunted her, as did Sweyn's failure to answer.

Sweyn came back carrying a woman's headrail—blue like Juliana's mantle, finespun and voluminous—a better garment than any she wore. Mutely she took it. She did not inquire whose it once had been, how he had come by it.

"Cover your hair—and keep it covered," Sweyn ordered. "Try to hide half your face."

Juliana obeyed, suddenly remembering Rhonwen's voice snapping the same order, and Marion transforming herself astonishingly with only a headrail, a stoop, and a shuffling walk.

"Yeh-so. Good!" Sweyn said. "On the roads you will be Wulfric's mother—or even the mother of his mother. Remember it."

"And once in Canterbury—when Wulfric is safe in Edgar's hands—what will I do then?"

Sweyn frowned impatiently. "No doubt Edgar—"

"Edgar will have no place for *me*! Where shall I go, if not to Winchester?"

"Jilly, how can I know that? There are nunneries."

Nunneries? The word echoed in Juliana's mind as she stared at him in disbelief. Nunneries were havens for the devout, for those who loved praying and meditation and humbling themselves in hopes of sainthood, and cared for nothing else. They were also convenient middens for unmarriageable daughters, undowered sisters, and unloved kin. Sweyn knew well that she had no gift for holiness, nor any taste for humbleness and seclusion. So what could he be saying?

Before she could frame a question, she felt his attention shift away from her. He was looking down toward the two gateway birches, where men and horses had begun to gather around a big white-haired man. Wulfric asked quickly, "Are we soon to leave?"

"Only I, today. You must wait. You'll be safe enough here—and safeguarded. Beorc has given his word on it." With a glance at Wulfric's face, Sweyn added, "Whatever you think of him, little monk, his word is good."

"But are we to kick our heels a whole day—" Wulfric was beginning, when Juliana cut in, her heart suddenly beating fast, as if she were running.

"His word is better than Harold Godwinson's?" she demanded. "Do you make Beorc swear on his own word, too, as you made me?"

Frowning, Sweyn half-turned away from her. "Jilly, swear as you choose. Forget I spoke of it."

"But you did speak. And I cannot forget."

"It seems plain enough. Father's sword was broken. So was Harold's word."

She studied his profile, feeling it hard to breathe. "What are you—saying?" She choked on it. "*You* believe Harold Godwinson an oath-breaker?"

"I think I must, my sister. Come—it is past and done with—"

"How can you speak so? I have heard such talk from

85

ignorant maids—from know-nothings whose fathers did not serve him—fight beside him, as ours did—"

"Jilly, you know nothing either." Sweyn's voice had roughened, but he spoke quietly. "He was a great lord, the gold-friend of warriors, I know that. But he took one oath he could not keep."

Wulfric made an impatient noise. "Explain your riddle, now you have gone this far!"

"Then listen, both of you." Sweyn faced them squarely. "Two summers before the ships came—in the time of old King Edward, who was ever fond of Normans and Normandy—in that time Earl Harold crossed the sea to William's duchy. Many say the king sent him. None can say why. But the king's nephew is the Aetheling. He was scarce older than Wulf then, and England had need of a strong man. It is thought Harold bore the king's promise to name William heir to England's crown—and himself took oath to uphold it."

For an instant they only stared at him.

"'Many say!' 'It is thought!'" retorted Juliana. "What truth in that?"

Wulfric said, "It can't be so. The king named Harold Godwinson heir—on his deathbed! Father told me himself. Well, everyone knew he would. And the *witan* approved it, and all the counselors and earls and everybody. *Father* told me, Sweyn!"

"And it is truth. And Harold put on the crown. But it is truth also that he bore arms in Normandy for Duke William. And swore fealty. That is known."

Juliana absorbed the shock, rejected it at once. "No man can know that!"

"Many do! His own warriors, who stood beside him, who helped him capture a castle in Brittany—for William—they know. They saw. We have three such, here in our camp."

"I cannot . . ." Juliana could barely speak. She felt as if all she had ever clung to and believed was being stripped off her just as Beorc had stripped her mantle.

Wulfric broke in. "They saw him *swear?*"

"They did so. In a place called Bayeux. There were two tables," Sweyn went on inexorably. "Two boxes on the tables—a rich cloth thrown over each. Harold Godwinson stretched out both hands and took oath on those boxes to call William lord. All the company saw—William's men and Harold's own."

"And in the boxes?" Wulfric persisted.

"Holy relics of Bayeux. The bones of saints." Sweyn drew a long breath. "It may be he did not know until afterwards—that he swore on relics. William may have tricked him. But he swore. He was too ready to take oaths, Harold Godwinson."

Juliana had a sensation of falling through the silence—down, down, with nothing underneath. The long-haired star—evilest of omens—streaked again through the darkness in her mind. "Yeh-so! He was tricked!" she gasped. "It may be he meant to call William lord in Normandy—but never in England!"

"A man's lord is his lord, whatever the country," Sweyn said flatly. "As I said, it was an oath he could not keep."

Juliana burst out, "Then how could it be—be—"

"Binding? I think Harold Godwinson felt it so—and considered it broken." Sweyn's eyes glazed with memory, with the haunted look she had seen that day in the forest of

87

Andred when his wound was new. "Jilly, a messenger from Duke William came—a monk of Fécamp—when we rode with Harold toward Hastings. And Harold changed. From that hour. The battle for England . . . he put it in God's hands. If he had *fought*—as men say he fought a bare week before at Stamford Bridge . . . But he did not even wait for the *fyrds* to gather in force. He did not order attack. There were so few of us—yet scarce room to swing an ax . . . All day we hacked and fell, crowded together on that narrow ridge, and in the end he fell with us. I think he left God to give victory, to judge him right or wrong to wear the crown. Yeh-so. And God judged."

Juliana choked, "I don't believe it. I will not believe it. I cannot understand."

"Nor did I, on that battlefield. Nor can I still."

After a moment Wulfric stammered, "I have heard . . . the Normans carried a banner sent by the pope. That the judgment was . . . because of the people's sins."

"A priest's answer," Sweyn said shortly. "Unless you think Normans sinless . . . Now in God's name let us talk no more of that day, only of this one." He glanced again toward the birches and the big white-haired man, who was waving. "I must go. Tomorrow—or when I can—I will take you to the road."

"Sweyn—wait—"

"Jilly, I have duties. There is food—you have only to ask. But do not leave the camp." He was gone. A few moments later men and horses had vanished behind the birches.

Juliana sat numbly, struggling to think no more of Harold

Godwinson, of the ill-omened comet, the striped ships, the lost past—the unknown future—trying to remember that Sweyn was Sweyn still, and to recapture the way she had felt only an hour ago. It was hard.

He will not—cannot—look after us, she thought. He has not told me what to do—except take Wulfric to Canterbury. After that I may go where I will—except not to Uncle Robert. *There are nunneries.* He cannot really fix his mind on me, or care for more than a moment. It is the camp's safety that concerns him. And his ravens. Those alone.

Sweyn was not Sweyn still, he was a stranger.

The camp settled into a tedium of waiting that lasted all day. Women moved about small tasks, their children played among the ferns, men mended leather or honed swords. The two deer roasted slowly on their spits, the nearest tended by a boy scarcely older than Wulfric, who wore a man's overlarge tunic, a dirk in his belt and another in the cross-gartering of a leg. Juliana saw Wulfric scowling toward him and said, "Let us walk about a bit—if your knee is rested."

Wulfric scrambled up at once. "It is over-rested—and so am I." As they started across the hillside toward the old bloomery-hearth he said, "In God's name let us get away from here tomorrow. I wish we had never come."

I, too, was in Juliana's mind, though she said only, "We must wait for Sweyn."

Wulfric began to talk of ink and pens, of Canterbury and Christ Church School, as if possessed by the thought of them. She murmured agreement to all he said, trying hard not to wonder where and to what bloody encounter Sweyn might be riding now, how it would feel to fight beside him.

They looked awhile at the old smelter, kicked at the weed-grown diggings, then wandered down the slope and in self-conscious silence around the clearing, avoiding the occasional curious glance while stealing their own at the men going about their tasks. They were of varied ages, and differing speech-ways—some with the accents of Pevensey, many more with the odd phrases of Finn and other Hastings men. Few had the clumsy build of humble cottars like Oswig, or the mien of swineherds or servants; most bore themselves like free villagers, even thanes. Oswig and his kind had stayed with the land, Juliana realized. It was their dispossessed masters who were here—or dead. She recognized no one; for the most part she and Wulfric were ignored as they pretended to ignore the rebels. By the time they had received food from the impassive boy-warrior and carried it back up the hillside, Juliana felt of so little account as almost to be invisible. However she might long for it, she had no place in the world of the camp.

It was dusk before the men came back, stained and weary, leading one of the big Norman stallions and the pony of the big white-haired rebel, who did not return. Half an hour later Sweyn climbed up the slope and dropped down beside them, bread and meat in one hand, a mug of ale in the other.

"You have had food?" he asked.

"We are well-fed. Sweyn, what—?"

"You must sleep well, and early. I will wake you near midnight—by the hour of matins at the latest—and take you to your road on the way to mine. By dawn we will all be gone from here."

"You, too?" said Wulfric in surprise.

"Men, horses, all." Sweyn's voice was taut, his eyes preoccupied in his thin-drawn face. He spoke swiftly, around his chewing. "We are disbanding the camp. Many like us are gathering beyond the Thames. We had word today."

"Gathering—for what?"

"To welcome the bishop when he comes to disperse us —as come he must."

"Bishop? Archbishop Stigand of Canterbury? That hermit told us—"

"No, little brother. Bishop Odo of Bayeux, Duke William's half-brother. *Count* Odo. Now Earl over Kent and half of Sussex. It's Lord Devil himself we hope to meet— prince of our ravens!"

Odo of Bayeux, Juliana repeated uneasily to herself. It was the first time she had heard the name.

They said their farewells and God-be-with-yous at a dark crossroads next morning, before cock-crow. For an instant Sweyn was Sweyn again, hugging them in his hard arms, his voice thick as he muttered, "God knows if we will meet again. Be wary, Jilly—keep your head covered. And your knife sharp, little monk. If ever you see our mother . . . if she still lives . . ." He hesitated, and Juliana knew he was thinking of Uncle Robert. "You had best say I am dead," he finished. A last swift grip on their shoulders and he moved abruptly to the ponies that had brought them. She

91

heard his saddle creak in the darkness, a faint jingling of bridles. Then he was gone, along the road that branched away northwest toward his waiting comrades and the hoped-for bloody meeting with his Prince of Ravens.

May God let the blood be this Bishop Odo's and not his, Juliana begged silently. Aloud, she said only, "So, Wulfric. We have our road," and resolutely turned northeast.

It was not the road the long-ago Romans had drawn straight as a ruled line through the pathless Weald. Sweyn's fox's knowledge of the forest had brought them out just short of Ashford-town on the Great Stour River. This road, barely visible in the pre-dawn, was a deep-worn track meandering in the Saxon way through a string of towns and villages, rutted with wheel-marks, pocked with hoofprints in the hard-dried mud.

Before full day they began to see other people—first only a dim, plodding shape or two ahead or behind, then more and more until the road was like an ant trail, one line of travelers brushing past the other as they hurried in opposite directions. Now and then the ants scattered as before a housemaid's broom when a pair or trio of mail-clad Normans cantered down the road. Then they clambered out of the ditches and struggled on. As Sweyn had said, half the world was trying to go somewhere else—and the other half trying to go about its work as usual, Normans or no Normans.

Wulfric said, "How long till we get there, d'you think? Two days? Three?"

"God willing, no longer," she assured him, though she was sure of nothing. "And may He give his help," she added under her breath.

God was unhelpful but in the end willing. Not three but five difficult days later, at mid-afternoon, a slight, stooped woman of indeterminate age, muffled to the eyes in a bedraggled blue headrail and holding the elbow of a badly limping ten-year-old boy, walked through the southeast gate in Canterbury's wall, called Worthgate, and into the town.

S E V E N

JULIANA KNELT ON THE WORN STONE STEP, THIRD FROM the bottom, with her back to the dim, death-cold reaches of the crypt. She was scouring step four with a handful of damp sand, trying in vain not to scrape her already raw and reddened knuckles against the gritty riser. Straight ahead and above her at the top of the short flight, Count Hugh de Montfort, sheriff of Canterbury, knelt facing her with piously clasped hands on the reed-strewn floor of the church's nave. Juliana eyed him with curling lip. No doubt he sought blessing from the Irish hermit St. Fursey, who was buried down here. Or perhaps he prayed to the bones of St. Wilfred in the High Altar, or to St. Dunstan's in the sanctuary just over her head. A Norman hypocrite—affecting to pray to Saxon saints.

As well pray to me, she thought, backing one step down to begin on step three. May the good saints scorn him as he deserves! *I* would send a plague of wasps to crawl under that great cloak of his and send him screeching out of here.

But her gaze clung to the thick, new wool of the cloak, which spread wide over the floor around his knees. It was dyed a yellowish green, which she was glad to note ill-became his sallow complexion, but bordered with embroidery—skilled Saxon embroidery—which would have lent elegance to a squint-eyed troll. He looked rich, well-fed, and warm. So warm. She could see a woollen tunic under the woollen cloak; close-woven linen next his skin showed at throat and forearms. As he rose and crossed himself, flicking bits of winter-dry rushes from his knees with a well-gloved hand, he revealed bowlegs encased in heavy woolen braies, snugly cross-gartered and ending in stout-soled, ankle-high boots. He pulled up the cloak's hood, which was lined with dark fur, and stalked out of her line of vision.

Juliana backed downward, grabbed an icy handful of sand out of her bowl, and began to scour step two. She herself was poor, ill-fed, and as cold as the old hermit-saint in his tomb nearby. The clothes Nurse Editha had put on her that bright dawn of Michaelmas Eve, 1066, were stained and threadbare in this bitter December of 1067. Outgrown, as well—tug as she would, the *rocc*'s sleeves would not cover her wrists, much less her ever-chapped hands, and the old mantle was near to rags. The warmest garment she owned was the thin wool headrail Sweyn had found for her; it swathed her head and shoulders at all times. As for the shoes of Queneva the ale-wife's dead daughter, they were worn clean through—useless, save for cutting into patches to mend Coleruna's, the old woman she had found shelter with. Juliana's feet were padded and bound in straw.

In vain she reminded herself that she ate daily, if not heartily, and that she slept under a roof—though it was only Coleruna's mud-hut thatch, and she must tend the old woman day and night to pay for it. She freely admitted that it was more than many of the drifting, homeless Saxons crowding Canterbury could boast of—or hope for, either. But they would not have been homeless—nor she, either —were it not for these warm-clad Normans she resented with a fury that seemed to grow, not fade, with every cold and hungry day.

I should never have stayed here, she told herself wearily, not for the first time. I should be in Winchester with my mother. But how could I go there without going to Uncle Robert?

Sweyn had forbidden that. Even Edgar had forbidden it, though for different reasons. And at the time, she had been more than glad to put off journeying anywhere at all, even wondering if in Canterbury she might find her own place, her own life.

Canterbury itself she liked well—in summer. It was a busy, important town, full of comings and goings—and in summer she had kept careful watch of them, half-expecting each day to glimpse a familiar face, catch a familiar Sussex accent among the Kentish ones. It was Edgar who had wakened her expectation. Shocked at her intention of leaving at once for Winchester, he had forbidden it in their first conversation, stating in his measured, positive way that she need not search for her mother, in Winchester or elsewhere.

"She is searching for you, Juliana," he had assured her. "More than a month back, a messenger came to me from your uncle. I could tell him nothing of you then, for I knew nothing, but—"

"So she is alive? You know this? She reached Winchester?"

"She did—at Eastertide, with Ragni and her servants, after long illness at a small nun's minster somewhere along their road. I believe the nuns did their best for her, and now she is cosseted certainly, in your uncle's care. You have only to stay here, and she will find *you*. Yeh-so! You must not wander alone about the countryside in these dangerous times. Your uncle will send again. *He* can give Norman safe-conducts. As even our prior cannot," he added a little bitterly.

"He is right, Jilly!" Wulfric had exclaimed. "Uncle Robert will surely do so."

He would, certainly. Once their mother had reached him, he would unfailingly have taken her affairs into his own firm hands. Juliana had stood silent and travel-weary, thinking, *I need journey nowhere, decide nothing*, and cautiously tasted the blissful relief it brought her. Moreover she was still free, for a time, of those firm Norman hands, and even, by some miracle, might evade them yet.

So she had stayed in Canterbury, expecting while dreading to see Lustwin's face, but in her heart believing that Edgar would soon send for her, the safe-conduct would appear, and her future would be settled willy-nilly. Exactly when belief had faded, when scanning new faces, listening for old accents, had become mere habit, she could not have said. But with the autumn rains and Martinmas the stream

97

of travelers had dwindled to a trickle. By now the roads were impassable and she was again a prisoner—again a drudge. This was hardly the miracle she had hoped for. Washing clothes and scrubbing church floors was little better than emptying slops and plucking hens. It took all her will to listen to Wulfric's eager prattle about his books and his new life, and keep her tongue between her teeth.

She scoured the final step, rose stiffly, and tucked both gritty hands in her armpits for a moment trying to warm some feeling back into them. The crypt had been chill last summer, when first she swept it; today, St. Nicholas Day, its cold struck straight to her bones.

Far above, in the north tower, the bell rang for terce. As quickly as she could, with her fingers numb and feet made huge and clumsy in their straw wrappings, she swept the scattered sand into its bowl with her faggot of broomtwigs and climbed the steps into the high, timber-framed nave. A backward glance showed her a stair of smooth-scoured stones, hollowed in their centers by centuries of monkish footsteps but clean and white—as ordered.

Orders had been flying everywhere about the monastery since first light. It was Rufus, one of the older novices, who had delivered hers. The prior had received his straight from Odo of Bayeux—Sweyn's Lord Devil—whose henchman had ridden hard from Dover, through the sleet-spitting pre-dawn hours, to deliver his command.

The command was to have the cathedral and all its precincts ready for King William's attendance at a holy mass —no one knew which one—sometime within a se'n-night; no one knew which day.

Eight months had passed since William had sailed to Normandy, taking with him Archbishop Stigand, an abbot or two, the three Saxon earls still alive—even young Edward the prince, the Aetheling—and anyone else around whom a strong rebellion might have formed. Scores of scattered ones had flared up everywhere during his absence; Sweyn's was not the only company of raven-hunters. Those in Kent alone had kept Lord-Devil Odo busy. But with no Saxon earl to unite them, no rightful prince to gather around, the fires had burnt out as quickly as they had flared. Now the striped ships had been sighted from the Dover cliffs, skimming toward Sandwich in a southwesterly wind. William was back at last from his long triumphal parading of captive nobles through his duchy.

Juliana wished he had stayed away forever—or sunk without trace in the gray, cold seas. Though as God lives, she thought, King William's foot on our necks can scarce be heavier than this Odo's set over us as earl!

Anyway, the crypt steps were fit now for an angel's feet, let alone a devil's, so her task was done. The first monks were already shuffling in through the northdoor and up the five steps to take their places in the stalls of the choir. She slipped out past them, across the shadowy vault of the tower, which still quivered with the deep voice of the bell, and outside into the cloister.

Among the nearest benches a confusion of schoolboys, of varying sizes but identically red noses, milled about old Brother Odbold. Stacking their writing-boards with a clatter that kept him hissing like a flustered gander, they gradually sorted themselves into a ragged line along the roofed alley. As she edged by them with her sand-bowl and broom Wulfric materialized from the hubbub and grabbed her sleeve, tugging her with him behind one of the timbers that supported the cloister thatch. His old mantle had been replaced by a warmer, larger one, coarse but still sound, outgrown by some older pupil.

"Meet me in the outer courtyard?" he whispered. "After Morrow Mass—when the brothers are all in chapter."

"It's St. Nicholas Day. There'll be extra services."

"Not for us boys. Did you hear the king was coming?"

"Oh, I heard," Juliana assured him bitterly. "No doubt the fleas in my bedstraw have heard by now. But I can't come back, I'll have old Coleruna to tend, then I must fetch the wash-water."

"Fetch it from Sunawin's well, just outside the gates here, and I'll slip out! Please, Jilly, I have a thing I must tell you—" Wulfric broke off as one of his schoolmates beckoned him urgently.

"Well-so, I'll come, I'll come," Juliana promised, giving him a shove. She watched the line of boys—Wulfric dashing for the tail end—file across the wintry open square of the garth. They were heading for the warming room, she noticed with the flicker of jealousy she would not own but could not rid herself of. A fire burned there all winter, so Wulfric had told her, in a big iron pot. The boys would be given a quick meal—bread and a mug of ale—and allowed to thaw their toes and fingers and noses until the bell ending terce summoned them back to the church to join the brothers at Morrow Mass.

She headed for the outer court trying to put down the

100

resentment she could no more help than hunger. It was well enough for him—fed and clothed and doing exactly what he longed to do. But what of her, pray? *It is not Wulf's fault, it is mine, mine.* she told herself vainly as she lumbered along past the sere gardens with what haste she could make on her huge-bundled feet. *No doubt I should not have heeded him, never even started for Canterbury.* But she had started, and had got him here, as she had promised. And they were well cared for, well treated, the Christ Church School boys—as Edgar had promised. She doubted that Wulfric would notice if they were not. It would take starvation and daily beatings to break through his joyful preoccupation with the reading, learning, pen-practice, words, and writing that now filled his life. This urgent thing he had to tell her would have something to do, certainly, with ink and quills.

In the small hovel near the monastery's grain-barn where the mops and scouring reeds and such-like stores were kept, she rid herself of her broom-faggot and bowl of sand, nodding to the stoop-shouldered young woman—clumsy on straw feet like her own—who earned bread for herself and her crippled infant by having charge of the place. Then she went on, hugging her freed hands under her arms, to the gatehouse.

Brother Godwin, the porter, was busy with a trio of nuns just arrived from somewhere with their grooms and their weary little donkeys, seeking shelter. When he had sent them off to guesthall and stables, he beckoned Juliana and fetched out the soiled laundry the infirmarer had left for her—a small bundle, she was glad to see—none of the heavy tick-covers that would not dry in cold, damp weather, drape them as she would around Coleruna's little fire-pit. Most of her washing this season was for the old or ill in the infirmary. The rest of the brothers seldom changed clothes in the winter—as indeed, who did? Old Coleruna had to be coaxed to do so even in August heat. She was *a-cold*, she would whine, pulling as far away from Juliana as her braided straw trucklebed would allow. Oh, it was a risky thing to take off one's bedgown! Jilly was a-cruel and unChristian to make a poor woman do so—Jilly meant to steal it herself, she did . . .

Wishing old Coleruna at the bottom of a well, as she did frequently, Juliana swathed herself more snugly in the blue headrail, settled the bundle on her head, and walked past the gatehouse, again tucking her hands under her arms.

To emerge from the walled enclosure of the Christ Church precincts was to step into the bustling market center of Canterbury. Crossing Burh Street into Mercery Lane, Juliana threaded her way past the stalls of mercers and saddlers, lorimers and smiths. Shops like cupboards were set into every house wall, with the carts of fishermen, salters, ironmongers slanting every which way among them. The frosty air rang with haggling voices, and smelled of horses and eels and humanity.

Dodging nimbly to keep the bundle balanced on her head without taking her hands from her armpits, she passed St. Andrew's Church door and the row of old Roman baths, honeycombed now with shops. Then at last she was free of horse and foot-traffic, and beyond the end of Hawk's Lane could climb the stile into the little meadow where the woolmonger kept his sheep. God knew the beasts had precious little to eat now, but they huddled, heads down, draggled and stained in their December wool, nibbling what they could. Beyond them, in the curve of the old amphitheater, traced now only by the tangle of ivy that grew from its crumbling walls, was old Coleruna's hut.

Juliana lowered the bundle from her head, ducked under the low thatch, and started down the three earthen steps to the dugout floor. On the second step she halted, still bent almost double, blinking into the dim interior. Something was different. As her eyes adjusted to the gloom she made out a hunched figure on the stool beside Coleruna's bed, where she herself always sat to feed the old woman her gruel. Sitting there now was a young woman cradling a baby within the folds of the headrail that swathed them both. All three faces—the stranger's, the baby's and Coleruna's—were turned toward Juliana, pale still moons, oddly wary, against the smoke-blackened wall.

"There you are, then." Coleruna's querulous voice sounded wary, too—then turned defensive. "It's Aelfwynn, Jilly. My own daughter's daughter. Journeyed all the way afoot from Fordwich, she did, and with the babby to carry."

Fordwich—an hour's walk, on an easy road. Juliana came down the last step, bracing herself inwardly for whatever was to come.

"There's Normans took over the master's manor. They turned her out from her place, they did. She'll have to stay here now, Jilly, and look after the babby and me too." Her thin fingers twisted the coverlet. "I've sent to tell Brother Siward. You must find someplace else to live."

103

After a moment Juliana put her bundle down. Then she picked it up again, looked at it half-seeing—and from it to the upturned buckets in the corner, to the fire-pit. "Will I not do this washing, then?" she heard herself saying numbly.

"Not here, child! You must ask the monks, not me. Ask your kinsman. Brother Edgar. Go along now, do."

The woman Aelfwynn said nothing. The babe in her arms blinked into space. Juliana turned and climbed back up the steps. There was nothing further to say. Brother Siward's rich Kentish kin had given the hut to old Coleruna, who had been his childhood nurse. Whatever befell their manor, the hut was hers; she could do with it as she chose.

It had all happened so suddenly that Juliana was halfway across the meadow before her mind moved beyond the immediate problem of the unwashed clothes she still carried, to the larger one of where she would sleep tonight, and how live without her laundering—without a fire to heat water, a bucket to fetch it—and the regular daily meal the laundering earned. Then panic seized her. *Go along now, do.* Go where? Back to Christ Church Priory, first, to hand back her bundle. After that—either join the hungry queue at the almoner's window, or thrust herself again into Edgar's unwilling hands.

I cannot do that! she told herself. I will set out for Winchester, winter or not, Uncle Robert or not. I will search for Sweyn, though he will not want me . . .

Certainly Edgar would not want her either. He was already cumbered with homeless kin—as were many of the Brothers. The Canterbury family of his mother's sister, summarily turned out of their fine house that Odo might present it to his knight Vital, were also hanging on his hands.

I am a burden, thought Juliana, suddenly humiliated beyond bearing. A burden to everyone, to myself. I must leave Canterbury today.

Pushing back across Burh Street, blind save to her own thoughts, she did not even glance toward Sunawin's well or remember her promise to Wulfric until she heard his hail and looked around to see him running toward her.

"Jilly? At the well, I thought we said . . . Where is your bucket?" He halted at her side, his bright blue gaze moving swiftly from her bundle to her face. "What has happened? You have not been home, then?"

"As God lives, I would I could go home! To *Pevensey*," she burst out.

"Pevensey is no home now," Wulfric reminded her. He pulled her out of the way of a donkey-cart. "Come—back inside the walls, where the wind does not bite so. Tell me."

The tale was soon told. Wulfric was silent—oddly unlike Wulfric—as he walked beside her to the gatehouse, where she gave up her bundle at the porter's window, bitterly aware that it would pass at once into some other freezing pair of hands, along with the meal it promised. Then he led her on into the great courtyard, to a bench set against the high wall.

"Edgar will say it is God's will," he said, in a voice as bleak as her thoughts.

"Edgar? Why?"

"It's what I had to tell you. He spoke to me. Yesterday.

105

When he came from chapter." Wulfric flung himself onto the bench, rubbed at an ink-stain on his finger. "The sub-prior and three other Brothers, with servants and baggage carts and all . . . they're traveling to Winchester. They're to bring back some abbot or other to await the archbishop . . . You may go with them."

"I? In such a company?"

"Among the servants. You would be safe, traveling so. Edgar will arrange it—if you want."

Juliana swallowed, moistened her dry, chapped lips. "I will go! God knows I cannot blame him if it is what *he* wants."

Wulfric shifted unhappily on the bench. "It is not what *I* want, Jilly." He flicked a doubtful sidewise glance at her. "No doubt you will be glad to leave. I know you are often hungry—cold . . ."

"I cannot stay longer. That is plain!"

He said sulkily, "God's will it may be. But I thought—I thought you would not want to go to Uncle Robert."

"Well, then—I do not!" Why do I fight so? Juliana wondered. In Winchester she would have food, warmth, lodging, servants . . . But they would be Robert fitzRobert's food, fire, house and servants. She could feel her jaw set. "No matter, I have no choice."

She met Wulfric's eyes—they were cornflower-blue above his wind-reddened cheeks, alert and searching. "Jilly? Are you saying . . . you *would* stay if you could?"

"As well say I would be pope if I could! There is no place for me here." Or anywhere, she thought desperately. Not anywhere at all.

"Go, then. I thought you would. But hark, Jilly! I have

106

been thinking, since Edgar spoke to me." He half-turned on the bench, peering at her intently. "Why could you not come back? In the springtime, when the roads are open. Bring our mother and Ragni with you, and Lustwin and Nurse Editha! Then we could live all together here, as we used to . . . well-so, not quite as we used to, but without Uncle Robert—"

"Have you run mad, Wulf? Our mother would never leave her comforts for a life like ours here!"

"It would not be like ours! She is not penniless, she took a great sack of something with her—depend on it, her treasures were inside! That great gold armlet Father gave her for a morning-gift, her jeweled brooches, that girdle with the fine silver buckle, no doubt a few pounds of silver pennies! How else would she have got the four of them from Lewes to Winchester? And what is left might buy a house here—"

"She would not even listen to such a plan."

"You could make her listen! Nurse Editha would help you, she had never any love for Uncle Robert! Tell her I wish it too! Tell her Sweyn wishes it—no, best not to mention Sweyn. But no doubt Lustwin—"

"You are dreaming, Wulf." She spoke the more harshly because he had set her dreaming too, asking herself if such a plan were possible, if one could gather the pieces of the old life, begin to put them together in a different way. It would be hard, precarious . . . But better Saxon hardship than hateful Norman ease. "I will—think about it. On my way to Winchester," she added bitterly. "When is this company leaving?"

"Soon. Within a fortnight—maybe two."

"A fortnight! I have not even a bed for tonight!"

Wulfric's face was still mirroring the hopeful images he had conjured up. "There must be a lodging somewhere. I will ask the almoner."

"I do not want alms! I am a thane's daughter!"

"*Tasks*, then. God's mercy, Jilly, put down your battle ax. I'll help. I will ask the sacrister, too—the guestmaster—"

For the sacrister she had scrubbed the crypt stair, in exchange for a loaf almost too small to remember. This talk is witless, she thought. I must find some prouder way to live, I will not cling another fortnight—two—on Edgar's charity!

She stood up, silenced Wulfric's eager, wishful planning with a cold finger on his lips. "Go now. Back to your pens and ink, before Brother Odbold comes from chapter and finds your desk empty. I'll—I'll ask the almoner myself."

She turned away quickly toward the gatehouse, heading for the almoner's window in the outside wall. Before she could cross the court a horseman clattered in through the gate, shouting something to the porter as he went by, and Wulfric was again at her elbow.

"It's the prior's courier, Jilly!"

"What?"

"That horseman—he was one of the lay brothers set to watch for the king's company. Quick! This one was sent down the Sandwich road—so they'll come into town through Burgate. We can see them all—the Aetheling, Earl Morcar, William too—" Wulfric was tugging her out the main gate, back down the crooked lane to Burh Street. "I'd like a look at King William once, wouldn't you, truly? If only to spit at him—"

It struck Juliana that she might already have had her look that black-omened morning as she stood on the shore at Pevensey, watching the striped ships sail in through the fog. One of those dark heads might have been his . . .

"Slower, Wulf!" she gasped as she stumbled and all but fell over her clumsy, straw-bound feet. Running at least started the blood coursing, bringing an almost-forgotten warmth surging up in fingers and cheeks.

Everyone was running, or starting to run, or at least staring at the runners and then walking, hobbling, or peering in the same direction, along Burh Street toward the town walls. Soon Wulfric was forced to an erratic, dodging pace by the numbers of people emerging into Burh Street from the lanes ahead. By the time they passed under the windows of the tiny church of St. Michael's, which bridged the street at Burgate, Juliana was breathless.

"Do you mean to run clean to Sandwich, or just halfway?" she demanded as they emerged outside the walls and Wulfric kept straight on, down Church Street St. Paul, alongside the long enclosure of St. Augustine's Abbey.

"Only to yonder tree." He pointed ahead, to an oak growing close to the high, thick abbey wall. We can climb onto the wall and see everything! Come along, it's easy!"

It was simpler to follow him than to argue—and possible, though scarcely easy, to mount the thick, bare branches of the tree to the top of the wall, which was rough stone but wide as a footpath. Juliana sank down thankfully, hugged her knees and tried to recover her breath. Her legs ached;

she had not the strength, these hungry days, to run so without tiring. Below in the street, people still hurried past, though many had begun to turn aside into the marketplace opposite—empty save on market days—where there was room to congregate and line the road. A few discovered their tree and joined them on the wall.

"No saying how long we'll have to wait," remarked Wulfric, but not as if it worried him. His own hopeful talk had restored all his normal high spirits. "Look, Jilly—down along past Newingate—you can see the castle from here." He was pointing southwest, where just outside the town wall, atop the ancient mound known as Dane Jon, the square wooden tower of Odo's castle rose—built in haste, hardly weathered yet—the mark of the Norman, the mark of conquest. "That's where the king will go first—you watch!—and later to the church to say his prayers."

"And may they choke him." Turning angrily from the sight of the Norman tower, Juliana found herself gazing—without seeing, at first—into the precincts of the abbey enclosed by the wall she perched on. Then suddenly she was seeing it, watching the Brothers, novices, servants by the score it seemed, coming and going between the abbey buildings. "Wulfric," she said. "Why should I not ask *there*? I might find tasks to do for the cook or the guestmaster—"

Wulfric followed the direction of her glance and glared at her, affronted. "At St. Augustine's? But we are of Christ Church Priory—Edgar and I!"

"What matter? This is a brotherhood of Benedictines like your own." Like, but larger, richer, older—the saint's own abbey, built first by his own hands when he came to pagan

England in a time beyond memory. His bones rested there still in the church of St. Peter and Paul.

"Jilly, we will find you a livelihood somehow. We at the *priory.* Edgar would never let you . . ."

Juliana wasn't listening, she was still staring over the wall. In that vast complex there must be a place for another pair of hands—for just a fortnight. A scrubber of steps, a scullery maid. God knew she was skilled at plucking fowl . . .

"There they come!" Wulfric yelled.

She whirled around, saw the glint of the first banners far down the road. On they came, looming larger and plainer, as those ships had loomed out of the fog, until she could make out William's leopard emblem fluttering from its standard over a jumble of men on tall horses. She found her throat suddenly closing and her teeth clenching. Normans. Conquerors. Murderers of her father and Harold Godwinson and her whole good, ordered life—what was she doing here, gaping like any simpleton?

"I do not want to watch them," she gasped, and stumbled to her feet.

Wulfric grabbed her mantle, pulled her down. "What ails you? You can't leave now, the wall is full of people!"

She watched in spite of herself, trying to keep her eyes toward the abbey courtyard, but finding them ever turning back to the cavalcade in the street. It came steadily, banners snapping in a cold breeze that brought a strong whiff of horses, saddles creaking and bridles jingling and the thud of hooves on hardened mud, with now and then a whuffling as one of the stallions tossed its head. A mutter of talk among the men who rode them—a company of shaven-

111

naped men in leathern armor, following a boy, three half-
ling youths, and several middle-aged tonsured monks, all
wrapped in rich short cloaks. In the lead, a dark sinewy
man with a proud eye rode alone. As he passed, the watchers lining the street, who had been craning and shoving
and chattering, grew still, as if a wave of silence traveled
with him down the road.

He wore a crown. Old King Edward's crown—Harold's
crown. William the Bastard, of Normandy.

He rode at a brisk walk between the rows of grim and
silent faces, heeding none of them. In his wake came the
boy with the three youths, and a voice or two called out,
"God go with the Aetheling!" or "God's grace on the Aetheling!" or "Hail to Earl Morcar! Hail Earl Waltheof!" The
third youth, then, must be Earl Edwin of Mercia, thought
Juliana with sinking heart. The last three Saxon earls, none
older than Sweyn. And that boy—a slim, pale child who
looked younger than herself—that boy was the Aetheling,
old King Edward's nephew, true claimant to Harold's
crown.

Small chance he would ever get to touch it, much less
put it on his head.

"That monk with the pig's face—that is Stigand," Wulfric
said in disgusted and quite audible tones. "Archbishop of
Canterbury! He looks like Father's old boar!"

"Hssst! Mind your tongue. His hand might be heavy on
the priory, now he is come home."

"He wouldn't know me again anyway. You can tell he
doesn't *look* at people, only stares them down . . . I told
you they'd head for the castle—there's Lord Devil coming
to meet them."

112

A second, smaller cavalcade was approaching along Broad Street, a wide road that bordered the town wall for half its circumference. In the lead was a black-browed, richly garbed figure who could only be Odo of Bayeux. Just short of Burgate, William reined his horse leftward into the broad way; the two groups met, paused, then moved together around the outside of the walls toward Odo's tower.

The watchers stirred and began slowly to disperse, their expressions inward. Juliana and Wulfric descended in silence from the wall and started back to the priory.

"An old, mean boar," Wulfric muttered. "And the king looks like—his leopard. And Odo like a wolf with its teeth showing . . ."

"They may look like hobgoblins," Juliana said bleakly. "They still rule England."

E I G H T

AT NIGHTFALL OF THAT ST. NICHOLAS DAY, CURLED UP among a score of other cold and unwashed paupers on the mildewed bedstraw of an almshouse, Juliana thought again of St. Augustine's. Edgar, caught at noon as he hurried across the cloister to sext and High Mass, had promised to arrange her journey to Winchester among the sub-prior's company, and somehow, with the help of God and Christ Church Priory, to look after her meanwhile. He insisted she need not turn elsewhere. For the present she must get daily bread from the almoner, and sleep in the priory's almshouse close outside the walls on Turnagain Lane—he could not say for just how long.

It will not be longer than this one night, Juliana vowed silently as she tried to curl herself farther away from the rank-smelling strangers on either side. Let Edgar say what he will, let Wulfric protest, I shall ask at St. Augustine's on the morrow. If it be slave's work, well, then, I will do it. Anything but alms and this stinking straw!

In a fortnight—or two—it would all be behind her, she would be on the road to Winchester. Instead of comfort, the thought brought a sinking, bitter feeling, which she tried to throw off. Is it not what I always intended? she asked herself. I must go to my mother, what else is there? Never mind Uncle Robert, I will not heed Uncle Robert, I will not mind what he tells me. There will be Nurse Editha, too, and Ragni and Lustwin—pieces of the old life—and, maybe Wulfric is right, maybe they will all come back here with me . . .

The bitter, dragging feeling remained. She could not argue it away nor put a name to it. But it felt like defeat.

She was wakened by St. Savior's bell, loud and close across the road, ringing, she thought at first, for nocturns. But it was too wild, too loud, too erratic—as if the ringer had tugged hard and frantically, then fled—and there was a growing hubbub of voices outside, in the lane. Around her, others were rousing, scrambling up to cluster around the unshuttered window—and beyond their heads, beyond the black silhouette of the priory walls, she saw the red glow lighting the sky.

There was fire—a big fire—in the monastery, it might be in St. Savior's itself. She stumbled to her feet, pushed her way out of the house. She reached the lane just as the bell ceased, and the north tower, which she could see now bathed in flames above the dark wall, collapsed with a terrifying, fluttering roar and a final jangle of noise. Wild with panic for Wulfric, she ran, heedless, for the main gate, found the gatehouse aflame, and turned back to run the other way, to the small gate by the cellarer's storehouse, which stood open, with figures crowding out through it, hampering her as she struggled past. Inside the walls, monks, guests, novices, schoolboys, ran in every direction, black shapes against the garish light.

She stumbled toward the day stairs, then swerved away instead toward the warming room, knew that was foolish and halted, half-sobbing and grasping after her scattered wits. There was no way to know where to search, he might be anywhere, he might be burned in his bed already . . . She seized the arm of one of the small boys rushing by, clung fiercely until he stopped struggling and turned a bewildered, frightened face.

"Wulfric! Where is Wulfric?" she demanded.

He shook his head, mouthing words she could not hear for the fire's roar, then tugged again and was free, darting away. She turned, watched for another boy, and captured him. This one only burst into tears and struck at her. The third waved his free arm toward a building behind him and shouted something. Under his other arm, as he pulled away, she saw the edges of a book. One of the Brothers dashed past him carrying a stack of them.

The library. They were trying to save the library.

She ran in the direction they had come from, uncertain which of the buildings housed the scriptorium and all the books Wulfric talked of, glancing fearfully over her shoulder at the blazing church to gauge the spread of the flames, dodging some of the hurrying figures and glancing off others, eventually colliding painfully with one—and it was Wulfric.

He was clutching two books and a roll of vellum, and fought blindly to get past her until she shook him and yelled his name. He stared a moment, then went limp and thankful, burrowing his head against her. Together they fought back to the gate and eventually through it. Once in Sun Street they turned to stare at the chaos behind them, both gasping for breath and Wulfric sobbing and choking.

"The church! It's ruined. The choir's gone. The nave's gone . . ."

And the bell tower, and the bell, thought Juliana, trying to believe it. After all these hundreds of years. Gone, without trace and forever, the ancient Saxon bones of St. Dunstan in the choir floor, of St. Oda and St. Wilfred and St. Elphege around the high altar. Gone, the altar itself and its treasured embroidered cloth, and the worn steps she had scrubbed that morning, maybe even the lonesome old Irish hermit in the crypt below.

If William had not visited Christ Church before vespers yestereve to say his prayers, he would get no second chance.

Wulfric's keening tally went on. "The prior's lodging'll be next, and the chapter house . . . and maybe the dorter and all our beds, though we saved some books . . ."

"How did it start?"

"Who knows? There was straw piled against the south tower. Some say a torch was left too near the cloister thatch . . . How does any fire start?"

In truth, how not? thought Juliana. The wonder was that

117

the church had stood so long, amid the fires that raced at intervals through Canterbury as through any town, at any time.

Wulfric's tear-strangled voice went on. "God knows what will be left. Or how they will keep the school now. Or where the prior is to shelter."

Juliana hugged him close and kept silent, her eyes on the flaring, hectic glow. God knows where *you* will shelter, she thought. Or Edgar—or that almoner who is to feed me. Certainly there would be no bread given at the window tomorrow or for days to come. Nor would there be a company setting out for Winchester in a fortnight or even a twelvemonth, to bring a visiting abbot here to this destruction. The future had again shrunk to tomorrow. And again, she did not know whether relief or panic was uppermost in her mind.

"Maybe the abbey will take you in," she said.

Wulfric went still, then twisted his head up to look at her. "Do you think so?"

"I do, then."

"*All* the Brothers?"

"All they can. Some Brothers have kin in the town, as well."

"Yeh-so! That is so. Some of the boys have, too."

It was an idea that fought gloom. Wulfric untangled himself and his books and vellum and stood again beside her, watching the flames. The heat was fierce on their faces, winter still cold on their backs. But there was no wind now, and presently Juliana felt the first drops of a quiet rain. God willing, some of the buildings would be saved, and the Brothers would manage somehow with what was left.

God willing. A few hours ago it had seemed God's will that she start for Winchester in a fortnight. Now, it appeared, God's fickle will had changed and she was to stay in Canterbury, with or without a living, with or without a bed.

So be it, then! she thought. But I'll have no more of alms or almshouses. As God lives, I will sleep in the meadow, rather, with the woolmonger's sheep! But I will sleep somewhere, I will eat somehow, they shall not defeat me again.

She did not ask herself who she meant by "they." She meant Normans—those bare-naped, leathern-clad marauders on their tall horses, and the crown-snatching man they followed. No matter that these flames were not Norman flames. No matter that it was old Coleruna, not Norman soldiers, who had deprived her of a roof this time. She would never have been under that roof, never in need, never facing a future as unintelligible as the marks on Wulfric's writing-board—except for Normans.

They will not stop me, she vowed again. I will find a future. I will make one! *Here*, then, if so God wills it! I will go tomorrow to the abbey.

N I N E

JULIANA STIRRED THE GREAT IRON POT OF OATMEAL POR-
ridge with a wooden spoon as long as her arm, leaning
perilously over the flames and clutching the handle with
both hands. Surely it had cooked enough; she could barely
drag the spoon through the gluey mass. Leaning the handle
against the pot's edge, she backed away, mopping her heat-
flushed face with an end of her headrail, exasperated that
she could tire of being over-hot when only a month ago she
had never been warm enough.

She turned to look around for Brighid, the abbey kitchen-
servant whose underling she was, and found the big Welsh
bondswoman already lumbering toward her, carrying a
stack of wooden bowls and shouting, "Well-so, it must be
finished by now, why have you not called me? Find the
lifting bar—there, behind you—wake up, idlebones!"

Brighid shouted everything; she was nearly deaf. And

she seldom said a gentle word. But in six weeks at the abbey Juliana had never seen her aim an ungentle blow or do a hurtful deed. All growl and no bite, she was, like the old dog who used to help the shepherd mind Baldric's sheep.

Juliana reached for the stout stick leaning against the fireplace and thrust it beneath the bail of the pot while Brighid set down the bowls to seize the other end. Together they lifted the kettle from fire to hearth. While Brighid packed the bowls—eight of them—into a basket, Juliana fetched a smaller pot and a wooden dipper, hoping, hoping.

"Well-so, fill it up, don't just gawk at it, they'll be a-hungered and a-starving afore you get food to them, pore squintin', scrunchin', sore-fingered souls . . ."

"I'm to take it to them, then?" Juliana asked breathlessly as she made haste to fill the small pot with porridge. It was best to be sure precisely what Brighid was ordering, for her tongue-lashings, while they left no more scar than a whipping with a thread, shook the rafters and one's composure.

"Was I not just saying so?" shouted Brighid. "Am I to weary myself with these comings and goings when the Holy Father's a-waiting for his boiled eels? Here, put a loaf or two in as well, must I tell you everything?" She snatched several little flat breads from the baker's shelf and flung them into the basket. "And don't be coming back here weak-kneed for lack of a bite of something, do you hear me? Stay there and pray a sup of theirs for once. It's nothing I've got here for the likes of you, and it's nothing you'll get. Now, begone!"

121

"I'm away . . . and I thank you, Brighid!" Hoisting the basket in one hand and the small pot in the other, Juliana hurried across the big, busy room.

Outdoors the January day was anything but over-hot. The light dusting of snow that had fallen during the night had crusted in the morning's cold, and the frosty air crackled in Juliana's nostrils. Crunching along the sanded way past the long front of the storehouse in her straw-stuffed, much-mended boots—once the property of Brighid's deceased brother—she wondered how Wulfric was faring in his new austerity. Gone were the days of comfort and plenty at Christ Church Priory. The Brotherhood, after a fortnight of camping out in the guest quarters of the Abbey, had managed to move back into their burnt-out buildings, but they were in sorry state. They had turned the former fraterhouse into a makeshift church, so must crowd instead into the kitchen for meals. The dorter had survived the fire, and part of the cloister alley between it and the frater—but many of the Brothers, Edgar among them, had found quarters in the town, since half the sleeping space in the dorter must now be used for chapter meetings, the infirmary, the sacrister's office, and God knew what else. The dozen or so boys who had no local kin to lodge with were crammed into a little house in Iron Bar Lane, and their schoolmaster, old Brother Odbold, lived there with them. And if they outgrew their warm clothing, they must go a-cold, because the chamberlain's stores had gone up in flames. Wulfric, having received his hand-me-down mantle only last autumn, was luckier than most.

And I, I am lucky too, thought Juliana. How long it would

last God only knew, but for now she was warm and housed and fed, thanks to the abbot who had set her to work here when they needed hands and rough-tongued Brighid who had kept her when the need was gone. Shouted down the cook himself, Brighid had, though she was a Welsh slave only, and spread a straw pallet for Juliana next her own under one of the big, scrubbed tables in the pantry.

Were all Welsh people rough-tongued and soft-hearted? Juliana thought of Rhonwen—who had looked after her, too, in that care-for-nobody way. And what had become of Rhonwen? Of Marion, and Queneva the ale-wife and her old mother, and Ulf the Miller and the widow Elveva . . . not to reckon Lady Edwina and all those others from another life.

Lady Edwina's image still lingered in her mind as she reached the north gatehouse at last. Awkward with her burdens, she edged into the narrow passage beside the gatekeeper's quarters and climbed the winding stone stair to the single long room set over the tunnel-like archway.

The buzz of conversation in the workroom broke off raggedly, and Brother Adam, the workmaster, pushed his stool back from the embroidery frame that stretched the length of the chamber, exclaiming, "Hail to Jilly!" Flexing wrists and shoulders, he limped over to meet her. "Now comes your midday, goodwives—and Brother," he added with a bob of his head toward old Cadwalla, the only other monk in the room. "Set the pot on the ledge yonder, little one. Let me take your basket. Come, friends, leave your work and to the table, rest your eyes and fingers."

Juliana hoisted the pot onto the broad window-ledge and

123

began to dip porridge into the bowls as Brother Adam held them out to her. He himself would eat nothing until after the three midday services, when the Brotherhood's chief meal was served in the frater. He was a quick-moving little man despite his lameness, half a head shorter than she was herself but thrice her age, with graying eyebrows as thick as mustaches overhanging twinkling little eyes. He always reminded her of some small animal peering merrily out of a thicket.

Stools scraped on the wooden floor and the talk rose again as the embroiderers hastily tied off a thread or took a half-stitch into the linen to secure their needles, and gathered around the trestle-table under the south windows, producing their spoons from various pockets in their clothing. Five embroiderers there were—three women and the two monks—as well as two wool-spinsters and the thread girl, Rosamond, who was scarcely older than Juliana, and always hung back to be the last to receive her bowl and loaf.

Juliana had not the knack of feeling humble. As Brother Adam came to the eighth bowl and hesitated, she gathered her courage and said, "I was told I might ask some."

"You shall, certainly!" he exclaimed, immediately handing her the bowl to fill. "Take one of the loaves as well, child. It is a good plan, eat while those you serve eat, then you may carry away the leavings—if there are any leavings! —and no need to make a second trip through the cold. But have you a spoon, or—"

The abbey bell, clanging sonorously for sext, drowned out the rest of the question, but Juliana answered by producing from the ragged pocket of her old mantle the wooden spoon that Wulfric had whittled for her last summer. Brother Adam gave her a nod and a smile, mimed a farewell to those around the table, and limped away down the stairs while the bell still shook the air in the workroom.

Brother Cadwalla sat on, placidly eating his porridge. He was too old, now, to stand for three hours, chanting, in a tomb-cold church. Along with other aged or infirm Brothers, he lived in the farmery, which had its own chapel and brief services, and he was excused from any labors more taxing than embroidery.

In truth, Juliana reflected as she filled her bowl, even embroidery might soon over-tax his failing vision. Twice of the three other times she had been allowed to carry porridge to the workroom, he had asked her—in a surreptitious whisper—to rethread his needle, and one of those times he had handed her wool of the wrong color.

Slipping a small loaf into her pocket and eating her porridge as she walked, she moved eagerly down the room, able for the first time to look closely at the partially worked embroidery. The design was drawn in watered ink on a long, narrow strip of fine linen, stretched at a slant for the convenience of the embroiderers, and lashed by sewed-on edgings, top and bottom, to the iron rods of the frame. The linen itself was scarce an arm's length from top to bottom, but from side to side it was longer than the room. The ends were rolled tautly around wooden poles—a lumpy roll of finished work at the left-hand end, a thinner one still untouched at the right.

She had never seen a like frame. Plainly it had been specially built for this ambitious work. Nor had she ever seen a like work—which was a continuous story told in pictures—though she had heard of such from Lady Edwina, who had seen similar hangings in churches or noblemen's halls or the palaces of bishops. There was a framed one depicting the Battle of Maldon of a hundred years ago and the valor of the Saxon leader Bryhtnoth. The embroidery had lasted to this day. Lady Edwina said it was Bryhtnoth's widow who had worked it with her own hands—no doubt assisted by her daughters and maidservants, just as Juliana herself, and Averil and Bernadette and the maids at Lord Alfgar's *burgh* had assisted Lady Edwina with her embroideries. Perhaps that new one they had planned to tell of Harold Godwinson's valor would have lasted a hundred years also—had they ever got to make it, had the striped ships not sailed into Pevensey and destroyed Harold Godwinson and changed the world.

This embroidery, too, was telling a tale about some ships. In the worked scene half concealed in the left-hand roll, she could see part of a striped hull, with a tall man standing alone in the prow and another just ahead in the water with his tunic tucked up high around bare legs. And there was an anchor . . . They were landing somewhere. But this was not a Norman ship, it was English, like the ones she had watched come and go since babyhood in Pevensey harbor. She could plainly see the special loading gap in the central gunwale planks, which Norman ships lacked. And besides, the tall man had a fine Saxon mustache, and no shaven nape. He was richly dressed, that man, in a nobleman's cloak fastened with a great brooch on one shoulder, and no armor, though he carried a spear. Her gaze clung to him.

126

"It is Harold," said a wavering old voice beside her, and she turned, eyes wide, to find Brother Cadwalla at her elbow.

"Harold Godwinson? Himself?"

"Himself. It is written there, above him, do you see?"

True enough, there was a pattern of black marks just above the embroidered figure—very likely they formed a word. Wulfric would have known that at once and could have read it.

"Then the tale is about King Harold?" she asked.

"It is about the four-and-twenty months before Harold became king, about a voyage he took to Normandy, an oath he swore to William—and about the battle at Caldbec Hill in which he died."

The monk's voice, thin and uncertain in pitch, was calm but sad, like his aging face. Juliana found her throat closing, angry tears stinging behind her eyelids.

"I have been told of that voyage—and that oath," she retorted, hearing again Sweyn's hard voice, saying, *Father's sword was broken. So was Harold's word.* "I do not believe it. I will not believe he broke his oath! The tale is a Norman lie."

"Softly, softly, God listens to such wild talk, my child," said the Brother with a smile that lightened his expression to its usual tranquil sweetness. "Brother Alain's design was guided by a life of King Edward being scribed at this moment by one of our learned Saxon scholars. A Norman lie that is not, certainly."

Shamefaced, Juliana muttered, "Yet your designer has a Norman name—Alain."

"Yeh-so, given him by his Norman father," said Brother Cadwalla placidly. "Husband to his Saxon mother, the Lady Edana of Sandwich. Brother Alain, too, was born in Sandwich, and has lived his whole life in Kent."

Half-Norman, half-Saxon, this Brother Alain. So would I have been, thought Juliana, had my mother wed that Norman nobleman Uncle Robert urged on her. "I suppose no man can help his name," she admitted, grudgingly. "His designs are fine, surely. As God hears me, I have never seen finer!" she added in spite of herself as she moved slowly along the frame, admiring the vigorously drawn figures, the groups of prancing horses, the hounds, the small animals running along the lower border—a goat, a sheep, a bull, a lion—the vibrant rust-reds and golds and greens —and above, more marks she could not read. "Is the tale about a hunt? I see two horsemen bearing hawks on their wrists."

"Ah, but they are prisoners," put in a new voice, a strong, clear tenor, from behind Brother Cadwalla. "Hounds, horses, falcons, huntsmen—and Harold himself—all captives of Guy de Pointhieu and his knights."

She turned quickly, and saw a monk neither old nor young, of high color, a tonsure fringed with black hair curly as a sheep's wool, eyes blue as Wulfric's own—and an air of exuberant assurance. Brother Alain himself, she knew at once. She drew breath, ready to defend her presence, but he gave her no chance, exclaiming to Brother Cadwalla, "Have we a new thread girl already, then?"

"Nay, Rosamond will be here yet a se'n-night. This is but the child who brings our midday. And now and again threads my needle, for its eye shrinks smaller every day," Brother Cadwalla finished with a rueful smile.

"But your skill does not, my old one," said the other, nodding briskly to Juliana and striding on, alongside the frame, sharply scanning the work.

"Rosamond will leave you soon?" Juliana found herself asking Brother Cadwalla in a breathless whisper.

"She will, for she is betrothed to the son of Widow Godeleva yonder, who spins for us, and they will soon be wed, and then she must look to her own thread-winding, and not ours."

"I will look to your thread-winding," Juliana blurted. "I can wind a skein before the next is half-spun—I have done so often—I am nimble and never drop or tangle, as God hears me—I can work hard, quickly . . ." She listened to herself, startled, thinking, *But what of Brighid?*, thinking, *Brother Alain will never allow it, I am playing the fool, I am tempting God.*

But Brother Cadwalla was smiling and peaking his sparse eyebrows, saying, "You, little Jilly? Well-so, you are deft of finger, certainly, and keen of eye. To that I can take oath. I will speak to Brother Alain if you wish it."

"Yeh-so, I wish it! If you would speak a word for my sake, I would thread all your needles, I would pick out all your snarls . . ." Juliana broke off, flushing. "No doubt *your* thread never snarls."

"Oh, does it not, then? There underneath the work, where my eyes cannot follow, and my hands become paws, and my back will not bend to let me look! Little one, I will speak to Brother Alain for my own sake!" Chuckling,

Brother Cadwalla turned his faded eyes toward the trestle-table, where his fellow workers were rising to go back to their stools at the frame. "Go now, child. I will see what can be done."

Hurriedly Juliana gathered bowls and scattered crumbs into her basket, and snatching the empty pot and dipper, made her way down the winding stair.

Her brain was whirling. Her own boldness shocked her—she had behaved as if she were Thane's Daughter still, confidently demanding what she wished. Her ingratitude shamed her—how would she tell her defender Brighid she meant to abandon her if she could? Yet she did mean to, there was no doubt of it. And then where would she sleep, if not under the pantry table?

Rosamond, younger than she was herself, yet soon to be wed—to the son of Widow Godeleva. Which was Widow Godeleva? The taller of the two spinsters, Juliana thought, the one with the sharp nose, and wiry reddish hair always escaping across her forehead from under her headrail. She was maybe not penniless, she and her son, only husbandless and fatherless. The battle of Caldbec Hill had left many fatherless—maybe Rosamond, too. But Rosamond had still a betrothed to secure her future.

Crunching across the frost-hard courtyard, Juliana thought for the first time in months of her own long-betrothed, Chelric, and the bride-gifts that would have been hers by law to do with as she would, but for Normans and their striped ships. *One pound of gold, thirty* hides *of plowland, twenty oxen, fifteen cows, ten fine mares, and six slaves,* besides the morning-gift Chelric would have bestowed on her after the marriage night—a fine gold ring or jeweled brooch.

It all seemed like an old tale—unreal, unbelievable, almost unimaginable. It belonged to a time that was finished, that would never return. Would not—could not, she realized, even if Saxons someday drove the Normans out. Nothing could ever be quite the same.

She halted, forgetful of the pot and basket dragging at her arms, of the iron-cold air and her numbing hands, while the knowledge spread through her with a chill finality. The past was—past. She had nothing left of it but Wulfric. *Now* was real—and only now. Ahead was nothing but what she put there herself, with the help of God and the saints. She could no longer merely live her life as it was ordered. She must order it, and she could not wait for her mother to come to Canterbury, or for that day that grew ever harder to believe in, when Saxons would take back their land.

She *was* ordering it, already—trying to climb from kitchen-slavey to thread girl, as she had somehow clawed her way to Brighid's warm kitchen from the almoner's window and old Coleruna's hut. Maybe—if she were allowed to serve as thread girl—she might one day be allowed to embroider. And that would be two scraps of the old life, Wulfric and embroidering, to build into the new. Farther than that she could not see.

Nor have I any need to, she thought as she came to herself with a shiver and hurried on past the storehouse. I am not yet even a thread girl.

T E N

BUT ONLY THREE DAYS LATER SHE WAS HASTENING JOY-fully out of the Great Gate between midday tasks and evening ones, slipping and sliding through thawing mud to seek out Wulfric at his books. Brother Cadwalla had spoken to Brother Alain; Brother Alain had said yes. She had not, it seemed, played the fool or tempted God's punishment. Clutching her ragged headrail around her shoulders, she turned into Church Street St. Paul and headed for the town.

She was forced to flatten herself against the abbey wall by a company of mounted Norman knights and their hangers-on, male and female, who were crowding their way toward the market on the other side of the street through the press of wheeled and foot traffic. Juliana watched them, wondering where their road might take them out of Canterbury, and thinking of Sweyn and his men, waiting somewhere to pick off ravens. The hunting would have been good the past month—and the danger to the hunters great.

132

Rumors came back constantly these days of the fierce fighting in Wessex, where King William was harshly subduing Exeter—and replacements for the men he had lost, well-armed like these, passed frequently through Canterbury, riding west. Staring at their Norman backs and wishing them ill-fortune, she was starting on her way when she caught sight of a female profile she knew well—one she had last seen framed by the hood of a torn and stained man's mantle, in Hastings castle. It was now outlined, snub-nosed and saucy, against a headrail of fine white wool, draped over a mantle of crimson pinned with a silver brooch. As she watched, the dark eyes turned her way, and Rhonwen saw her.

"God's mercy, it's Jilly! Wait, don't run away, let me look at you!" The Welsh maid—plainly, bondmaid no longer—spurred her mare out of the press and across the road to where Juliana stood. It was a fine mare, white as cream save for its mud-spattered legs, and wore a handsome worked-leather saddle. "So you did get away from that place alive—and all these miles to here, too! I gave you up, you know—a little know-nothing all alone!"

"I am not a know-nothing! Nor was I alone. My brother was with me."

"The big one? Sweyn?" Rhonwen's glance was running over her, and missing very little.

Juliana, conscious of her rags and straw-stuffed shoes, lifted her chin. "No. Wulfric."

"The more praise to you, then. I'd have taken oath the dogs would get you. But what are you doing in Canterbury?"

Yesterday, the humiliating answer would have been, *the*

133

same as I was doing at Hastings, but today she could raise her chin a trifle higher and say, "I am to help with a great embroidery at the abbey—while I am waiting for my mother."

"And where is your mother? And the little sister? They did not die in that fire, then?"

"They did not. They are safe in Winchester with my uncle."

"The Norman uncle? The boggart! So he had his uses after all." Juliana disdained to answer, which produced Rhonwen's old mocking but understanding laughter. "Come, I shouldn't tease you. I'm glad she's safe—and you, too, Jilly. God knows we've had enough to bear without picking at each other. But I've come up in the world while you went down."

"So I see! Did you find a Welsh elf's pot of gold?"

"I found a boggart of my own, little one. He was a knight at Hastings—a new-made landowner now! We're off to Oxford to take over his estates . . . Then God help me, for he'll summon his lady from Normandy, and I'll be out. Still, he's made me a free maid, and the mare is mine. No doubt I'll find another boggart."

"Normans! I wish you joy of them," said Juliana scornfully.

"God's mercy, Jilly, did Saxons ever give me more than bondage and beatings?"

"My father was a good master!"

"Well, Normans are everyone's master now—yours, too. Wake up, little ninny! The world is as it is."

Rhonwen smiled and reined her creamy mare away, toward the market, but Juliana, remembering the half-impatient care Rhonwen had always taken of her at Hastings, put a hand on her stirrup to stop her. "Beware of rebels—near the Weald," she said.

Rhonwen's dark glance met hers, and she nodded. "I will, then. My thanks, Jilly. God be with you." She nudged the mare and was soon lost in the crowd.

Juliana went on more slowly toward the walls of Canterbury with year-old memories sweeping over her. What had become of Marion, she wondered. She had not thought to ask. Very likely Rhonwen would not know, in any case, having got out as soon as she could and put the place from her mind. Was Hugo Mangebien still guard at the castle gates? Still strutting in that mantle embroidered with trolls and frogs? Juliana pulled her rags around her and straightened her shoulders. She might be doing the same tasks here as there, but she did them for Saxon monks, not enemies.

She passed into the town through Burgate beneath St. Michael's tiny church, and along Burh Street to Iron Bar Lane and the lodging of Brother Odbold and his pupils. It was a low, thatched warren, part house, part former stables. The latter, being half-open to air and sky, was the part best lighted and therefore served the boys as schoolroom, with mangers boarded over for desks. Passersby could peep in past the courtyard, and the boys could peep out—unless they were blind to all but their scribbling.

Juliana posted herself in her accustomed spot and waited impatiently, one eye on the lowering clouds and the other on Wulfric's red-gold head, half-visible behind a thatch-support. In a moment he leaned back, stretching, glanced toward the lane, and saw her. He was up in an instant, disappeared, reappeared in the stable doorway, and was soon leaping across the mud-puddles toward her, already talking.

"Jilly, guess who I saw—I *think* I saw—coming home from Morning Mass—he was just riding into Mercery Lane, there by the Forum, and I yelled like a banshee but Brother Odbold bade me hold my tongue, and by the time I'd explained, he was gone—I didn't see where—"

"But who? Not Rhonwen? You said 'he'—then it was Lustwin! Or one of Uncle Robert's—"

"Rhonwen? Who is Rhonwen? It was Grimulf, Lord Alfgar's reeve! Or his twin, I take my oath. Same bald pate, and humped back—I even thought his horse was that old dapple Chelric used to ride, but I only—"

"Grimulf! But then—but then—" Juliana broke off. But then, nothing. Grimulf in Canterbury—if indeed it had been Grimulf—did not mean, as it once would have, that Lady Edwina was in Canterbury, or Averil or Bernadette. In these scattered times it meant only that Wulfric had likely been mistaken. "Many old men are bald and stooped," she said. "Many horses are dappled. And Canterbury is a crossroads for all the world! I just saw Rhonwen outside St. Augustine's market."

"Who is—oh, that Welsh bondmaid?"

"A free maid now, and leman to a Norman knight, riding a milk-white mare and dressed like an earl's lady—on her way to live on stolen Saxon lands . . . for a little while." Juliana swallowed her anger, waved the meeting into the past. "I wish her no ill. May she prosper. Hark now—I have real news! I will soon be out of the kitchens—"

136

Eagerly she spilled out her story, and Wulfric's impatience to tell more of his own soon changed to startled attention.

"Do you mean—the great embroidered hanging? The one Brother Alain is designing?"

"You know of Brother Alain, then?"

"Everyone knows of him," said Wulfric in a tone as near to awe as she had ever heard him use. "Brother Odbold says no finer draughtsman has been known at Canterbury in a hundred years—at Christ Church or the abbey, either one. He showed us a book once . . . angels could draw no better."

Juliana blinked, impressed by Wulfric's deep respect. "The designs are lively, certainly. I have seen them." She added, "I saw *him* too, three days ago. He has hair like a black sheep's . . . He is half-Norman."

"What matter if he is half-troll, when he can draw like that? And *you* are to help in this work of his?"

"Why should I not?" demanded Juliana. "He must have needles and hands to use them—and mine are as skilled as many—more so than some working for him now! Though I will be only thread girl," she added, coming back abruptly to reality. "But I will have three silver pennies each month, Wulfric! I can find my own food, and need not put Brighid to the task of stealing it for me." She smiled, remembering. "I was ashamed to tell her, after all her kindness. But she wished me godspeed—that is, she shouted, 'Good riddance', and commanded me to sleep under the table as before—to guard the pantry from the rats, she said."

"You will not do that!"

137

"I will not, certainly. Brother Cadwalla has found me another bed, at his kinsman's—Toli the moneyer. There is a room in the attic they will let for a penny the month, and I may sup with the family if I scour the pots. I am to go there tomorrow."

"Yeh-so, good, then!" Wulfric was barely listening. "Jilly, all the scriptors are talking of that embroidery. It will be seventy ells long, maybe more!"

"What? It is not, then! I saw but a room's length—ten ells or so it may be, I could not see, since it was half-finished, and rolled at the ends—"

"But it is only begun! There will be other lengths—all sewn together when they are done! It will tell the whole story of Harold Godwinson, and the voyage to Normandy, and the oath Sweyn spoke of—"

"Yeh-so. The oath!" Juliana felt the familiar mutinous anger rising. "*That* does not please me. To be part of a Norman lie."

"Jilly, it is a great work! It is an honor to be part of it! *My* sister." He gazed at her as if trying to imagine it—a look half-envious, half-disbelieving. "I will boast of that to the other boys! I need not say you are only the thread girl," he added practically.

"I would gladly be sweeping maid—so long as I have the pennies. Or . . . I would not, then! I wish to wind the wool for that embroidery! Except . . . for the part about the oath. But Brother Alain would design it so!—being half-Norman."

"Huh! Half-Norman or full Saxon, he will design as he is told to, I've no doubt."

"But the abbot would not have him tell a Norman tale!"

Wulfric stared at her a moment, then his expression changed to a strange one, barely tinged with mischief. "Jilly—do you not know who commanded this great hanging?"

"Why, the abbot, I suppose. Father Aethelsige of St. Augustine's."

"Not so. It is not even meant for St. Augustine's, but for a big church a-building now in Normandy. In Bayeux."

"Bayeux?"

"Where Odo is bishop. Our own Bishop Odo, earl of Kent." Wulfric's rueful eyes met hers. He shrugged. "Lord Devil is Brother Alain's master. And now he's yours."

For an instant Juliana stood dumbstruck. "No!" she gasped. "I'll not have it . . . I'll not do it. I'll go back to the kitchens . . ."

"What? That's fool's talk! I should not have told you," Wulfric said penitently.

"I'd have found out, soon or late . . . But Wulf, I *cannot* go back to Brighid. The cook would never allow it . . ."

"Nor would I! Eating scraps and sleeping on the floor!"

"But what am I to do else?"

"What you wish to do, ninny! Live at Toli the moneyer's and work on the great hanging, and forget who is master!"

Juliana turned on him hotly. "How could I forget that? What would Sweyn say?"

"Sweyn is not here to say anything," Wulfric pointed out drily. "Nor did he say much helpful when he had the chance. Will you let Lord Devil stop you doing what you wish?"

That was another way of looking at it, indeed. "I will not, then!" Juliana flashed back. "No Norman shall say me yea or nay . . . if I can prevent it," she finished lamely. "But Wulf—I have had Norman masters. As you have not."

"Brother Alain is not like that! As for Lord Devil—I doubt you will ever set eyes on him yourself."

The abbey bell pealed through the cold air, sounding nones, causing both to jump and Wulfric to cast a quick glance over his shoulder. "Courage, Jilly," he said roughly. "*I* wished for Canterbury—remember? And here I am! What you did for me you can do for yourself. God b'with you!" And he was gone.

She stood a moment, staring unseeing at the wintry lane—rebellious, helpless—with the deep bell and Rhonwen's parting words echoing bitterly in her ears. *The world is as it is.*

Then, huddling her headrail about her, she started back toward the abbey to help Brighid one last time form the loaves for supper. The cook had decreed that morning must see her gone. He had shown mercy to let her stay so long. Tomorrow, whoever was master, she would wind the wool. She must not think of Sweyn or Odo. She must think only of courage—and of thread.

E L E V E N

THE WOOL WAS RUSSET AND BUFF-GOLD IN THE DYED, matted fleeces waiting in the corner, paler buff in the fresh-carded mass tucked under the widow Godeleva's arm, which flowed from her nimble fingers in a thin strand down to the wooden drop-spindle that whirled and tilted near her ankles. The spindle rose rhythmically to her hands and down again as she paced back and forth, spinning and winding, spinning and winding, passing and repassing young Ingold as she did the same thing—though not as expertly. The twisted thread deepened to gold as it grew around the widow's spindle and darkened its green around Ingold's. It shone rust-red in the fresh-spun hank Juliana was winding from skein to ball, her hands moving from one end of the skein-rack to the other, her wrists lifting and dropping. At the long frame down the center of the room, the single threads glimmered—fine lines of rust or buff-gold, one or

141

two pale green, as the embroiderers pulled their needles through the linen and to arm's length past their bent heads. And on the work in the frame, the colors slowly grew and spread into glowing patterns.

It was all like a ritual dance, each motion repeated in ordered sequence and none wasted, Juliana was thinking as she wound and watched. And the music they moved to was the deep voice of Brother Adam, who perched on the edge of the table in a shaft of pale spring sunlight and read to them from the history book of the saintly Bede. He was waiting for the dark green thread still on Ingold's spindle. Ingold's fingers were not as deft as Widow Godeleva's, and sometimes she dropped the spindle before she meant to, and must wind a length all over again, and sometimes while her fingers were busy pulling the thin strand of fibers from the carded hank on her shoulder, the spindle slowed and began malevolently to revolve the other way, untwisting thread already spun. Juliana knew all about the ways of spindles, and sympathized. She hated spinning. Ingold was far more deft than she, but still the embroiderers often had to wait in idleness for more thread.

They had need of a third spinster. Brother Alain had often said so.

Brother Adam's voice went on reading—a voice oddly booming for such a merry little grasshopper of a man. " 'Indeed, Your Majesty, the present life of man on earth seems to me like the swift flight of a single sparrow through the banqueting-hall where you are sitting at dinner on a winter's day . . . In the midst there is a comforting fire to warm the hall; outside, the storms are raging. Inside, the

142

sparrow is safe from the winter storms; then he vanishes into the wintry world from which he came. Even so, man appears on earth for a little while; but of what went before this life or of what follows, we know nothing . . .' "

The ball and thread in Juliana's hands blurred and swam as the hot tears sprang to her eyes. It was not the mystery before this life or the one after death that disturbed her, but the sudden picture, vivid as memory could make it, of just such a hall, with just such a comforting fire, even just such a sparrow fluttering from here to there among the rafters. Quickly she brushed away the tears, frowned away the memories, and went on with her work.

Brother Adam closed the book and returned it to its protective case as she came toward him with the new ball. "So. I will do the laid work on the red horse now, and leave the couching of the green till Ingold has the thread. You had better wind the buff next—we'll soon need more of it."

He went back to his place at the frame, and Juliana, idle until Widow Godeleva should have finished spinning the buff, walked slowly behind the embroiderers, studying the work sharply for signs of Norman lies. It was a new length, the second section of the hanging, that they were beginning on now. Already complete was the complex tale of Harold's journey into Normandy with his hunting companions, their capture by Guy of Ponthieu and their rescue through the aid of Duke William the Bastard. Only the decorative borders at top and bottom remained to do, and Brother Alain had sent the long, narrow linen, now bulky with embroidery, to the little nunnery of St. Agnes on the Sandwich road, where the many little beasts and birds and trees and fabled figures of the borders would be filled in more slowly by less-skilled workers.

The new section, lightly drawn in watered ink in Brother Alain's bold and vigorous style, would show William welcoming Harold to his castle (—and so he should! thought Juliana!)—and enlisting the help of Harold and all his men in a campaign against the Duke of Brittany. Further scenes showed Harold distinguishing himself in battle as well as rescuing Normans and their horses from the quicksands below the great abbey of Mont St. Michel. (And he would do so, certainly! thought Juliana. No one was stronger, braver . . .)

So much had Brother Cadwalla explained to her, reading out the inked-in captions that morning before work began. And she had felt quite kindly toward Brother Alain and his tale of Harold as it showed the Duke of Brittany surrendering, the battle ending . . . until there came the scene of William bestowing armor upon Harold—which in truth made him knight of Normandy and so William's vassal. This roused all her suspicions, though the dreaded scene of the oath itself, if such a scene there were, was still hidden in the rolled linen at the end.

Pausing now behind Brother Cadwalla's stool, she found him bent nearly double over the frame, reaching under with one hand, over with the other, plucking in vain at a loop of thread that had knotted itself somehow.

"Shall I help you, Brother?" she offered, and he straightened with relief, pushing back his stool to allow her to crawl underneath the frame. Cross-legged on the floor with her head cramped sideways and the threads only inches from her eyes, she soon found the knot and loosened it, scrambling out again to find him squinting ruefully at his work.

"Alas, I have sewn that spear crooked," he told her. "Do you see?—just there where it crosses the horse's breast. Does it seem to you it has a kink in it? I fear no one could bring down an enemy with that weapon!"

"The kink is small, Brother—surely it would never be noticed!"

"*I* have noticed. Well-so. I shall pluck it out, and do it over. I do not like poor handiwork!"

It was not his hand that failed him, but his eyesight, as they both knew—also that it was harder by far to pick out stitches than to set them. "Will you let me do it for you?" Juliana whispered, with a glance at Christiana, whose stool was next to his. But Christiana was a little deaf. "I can be here in the morning before the others, work swiftly, and no one will ever know. As God hears me, I can do it well."

"You can, certainly, or you would not have offered," Brother Cadwalla told her warmly. "You are a sweet child and a good-hearted maid. I accept your offer."

Her heart lightened by his praise—and by the prospect of serving him, for she owed him many kindnesses—Juliana hurried back to the far end of the room, where the widow Godeleva's hank of gold thread would soon be ready for winding.

At sundown, walking out the main gate with the braided clangor of Vespers sounding all around her, she found Wulfric leaning against the great wall, plainly waiting for her, though he was staring off into the distance, a strangely rigid look on his usually cheerful face.

"What is it? What is wrong?" she asked as she came up to him.

The expression vanished instantly. "Now why should you think anything is wrong?" he demanded. "I have found a better patch of scurvy-grass, and mean to show it to you. Come, it's yonder behind the Salt Hill market, almost to Newingate. God willing—I hope—not many will have discovered it yet."

"You should hope rather that there is enough for all," Juliana said severely, sounding even in her own ears like Nurse Editha. It seemed to her the monks' sanctifying daily influence was hard to see in Wulfric.

But he only retorted, "Well, so I do hope! But in case God did not sow it thick enough for all, we had best get there as soon as we can." As they started toward the town wall, he added casually, "I saw Edgar today after Morrow Mass. He said—" Wulfric fell silent an instant, striding along beside her with his eyes turned elsewhere, then finished in a rush. "He has had word of our mother."

Juliana stopped in her tracks and stared at him. "Why did you not tell me at once, simpleton? All this talk of scurvy-grass and markets—"

"Well-so, which comes first—to stop our teeth falling out today, or talk of something to happen a month from now?"

"What is to happen a month from now? Who is the word from? Is Lustwin here?"

"No. Give me time, I will tell you everything! Some bishop from Winchester—he is high up in the court there —came last week to see the archbishop. He talked to Edgar yestereve."

146

"Of us? Our mother has sent for me?"

"She does not even know you are here!" Wulfric reminded her. "Though she will, once that bishop goes home. Edgar told him of us—asked after her welfare . . . It seems she is well, indeed." Again Wulfric broke off.

"So? That is good news, surely? Why do you not go on?"

"Because you will not like it!" Wulfric burst out. "Nor do I. He says she is much seen in court circles—a prime favorite of the old queen."

Juliana stared at him in sudden foreboding. Queen Edith, Old King Edward's widow—Harold Godwinson's own sister —had been the first of the Saxon court to surrender to Duke William. Before ever he arrived in Winchester to take it, she had sent word to him in London that the town was his. "I knew it! Uncle Robert has surrounded Mother with Normans!"

"Edgar says it was only to be expected. Our Aunt Bergitta is one of Queen Edith's ladies. And now—our mother is also." Wulfric swallowed, then suddenly blurted it out. "And she is to be wed."

Juliana felt as if she could not get her breath. "What are you saying? Our mother? *Wed?* Edgar told you this?"

"The bishop told him."

"Well, it is a lie! She could not wed other than our father! She would not—"

"I said the same," Wulfric muttered. "But Edgar—talked to me. Our father is dead, Jilly. His lands are gone. She has nothing but a few bits of gold and silver. She is not like you—she needs someone to take care of her."

For an instant everything in Juliana cried silently, *I, too,*

147

need someone to take care of me! But the wave of discouragement, of weariness and bitter despair, passed, leaving her stiff with anger. "She has our uncle to look after her!"

"Yeh-so. Well, this is his way of doing it. The man is his friend. A Norman baron."

A Norman. The final shock went through Juliana like a chill, but she rejected it violently, gesturing with both hands as if hurling it away. "I don't believe it! An idle rumor! The bishop is a gossip-monger!"

"Do you think so?" Wulfric said hopefully.

"How can I know? Where is he, then? I will go myself—"

"He is gone. He left for London at daybreak."

"Edgar might have warned us!"

"He did not meet him until yestereve."

She drew a long breath, tried to think. "This is—to happen—a month from now?" It seemed very close.

"Soon after Easter—so that bishop said."

"But Easter is surely not . . . March has barely begun."

"Easter falls on the twenty-third day. King William's lady, Matilda, comes from Normandy to be crowned queen on Whitsun. The bishop says our mother and—and her new husband will go to London for the ceremonies. Jilly . . . suppose it is true. Does it not seem to you they will certainly come here before that—and take you away with them?"

"I will not go," said Juliana instantly.

"What if they make you?"

"They cannot! I will run away—to Sweyn, in the forest. Or hide somewhere . . ." She was talking wildly and stopped short. "I will not go a step with any Norman," she finished.

Wulfric scanned her expression for a moment and seemed to take comfort from it. "I hoped you would say that."

He must have known she would say it. But whether either of them believed she could make good her vow, she did not know.

They walked on. Juliana's thoughts felt like wheels in mud—slipping, locking, unable to move beyond *I will not go* to *How would I avoid it?* She tried to imagine the new husband, the new marriage, and found she could not even picture her mother's face. Nurse Editha's came quickly, clearly—and little Ragni's, with its frame of curls—but for a few moments her mother's eluded her. Then it was there, along with a rush of feeling, a tumble of memory—the pale slant of hair across the forehead, the headrail bordered with her family's pattern, the large eyes, gray like Sweyn's —like her own—but unlike theirs, always uncertain and slightly anxious. And Uncle Robert's dark and confident features loomed right behind.

Suddenly she found herself wondering why she had not guessed at this outcome, long ago. It was as if it were fated—perhaps it was God's will. The next instant she was rejecting it again: *I do not believe it, I will not believe it! It is not true!*

"The herbs grow yonder. Back of that falling-down shed. We will get muddy," said Wulfric absently. He had been stalking along in preoccupied silence. "Perhaps they will not make you leave, Jilly," he added with sudden urgency.

"You have a place to live now, and the thread-winding, and the three pennies every month. They cannot *drag* you away."

They could, but Juliana did not say so. Nor did she remind him that three pennies a month and a tiny loft would scarcely convince their mother that she was living a life suited to her birth or reassuring as to her future. She said only, "I will not go."

They tracked across the muddy waste-ground to the half-fallen shed and found the patch of green behind it. Others had found it too; a woman and child were there, plucking the herbs into baskets, and a man was just leaving with his sack full. But there was plenty. They bent to the welcome task, biting the tender ends off eagerly and then gathering more while they chewed—Juliana filling the looped-up end of her headrail, Wulfric his pockets. Each spring, the effect of the first greenery—scurvy-grass, new hawthorne shoots —was like a touch of God's finger. Within hours the aching teeth eased, the dragging weariness lightened.

When they had all they could carry, they turned again toward the town, passing through the wall at Newingate into St. George's Street. They said little, and nothing about Easter. But when they paused at the end of Iron Bar Lane, Wulfric scanned her face a moment, then said, "If it is true, Jilly, do you think our mother will let me stay here?"

"I do, then. She would not take you from your pens and books."

"Well, she could not, for I mean to take holy orders! I decided that long ago."

"Be easy. She will not try."

"Perhaps—it is all a rumor."

150

Juliana swallowed. "I will not believe it—until she comes here and tells me herself that it is so." She was suddenly thinking of Sweyn's careless words: *There are nunneries.* There were, indeed. Here, nearby. If there were no way left to her but Wulfric's . . . It was in God's hands.

Reluctantly they parted—he to his makeshift dorter with Brother Odbold and the boys, she straight on across the center of the town, down High Street past the pillory, turning off just short of the river into Hethenmanne Lane. Here, halfway down the little street toward the Hottewelle where she had so often drawn the water for her washing, stood the house of Toli the moneyer and his wife Audrey. It was a fair-sized house, with the workshop in the front half and living quarters in the back, and compared to Cole-runa's hut it was a palace. Until this day Juliana had been well pleased to live there, grateful to Brother Cadwalla and his kinsman Toli. Now suddenly she saw it through her mother's eyes and it was a poor craftman's dwelling, cramped and needing new thatch, lacking even the space for garden and pigsty possessed by the least of her father's tenants.

As she opened the back door Audrey straightened from stirring the pot of bean-porridge slung over the fire-pit, wiped her forehead with the tail of her headrail, and turned. The odd, down-slanted eyes in her narrow face went instantly to the greenery Juliana was turning out onto the table.

"You have found scurvy-grass! Take it into the work-shop." The eyes moved briefly to Juliana's face. "It is well you did not eat it all yourself. Leave me some for the child."

Biting back the vexation Audrey's shrewish ways always

roused in her, Juliana did as she was bid. Toli's wife did not like strangers in her house; she wanted the loft room for her loom, which was now crowded into a corner by the fire-pit, and did not let Juliana forget it. Monthly penny or not, Audrey would be happy to see her depart for Winchester. What her mother would say to Audrey, Juliana could not imagine.

Setting aside a handful of scurvy-grass for the sickly little Edana, she piled the rest into a shallow basket and carried it past the leathern hanging, through the dim earthy-smelling storeroom, and through the door into the shop, which she could hear well before she got there. Ordinarily she loved the shop, and often made excuses to linger there, watching. It was full of sound—the constant delicate pinging and tapping of hammers on silver, punctuated by the strong *thwack*-chink, *thwack*-chink on the die as Goldwin, the apprentice, stamped coin-blanks one by one and tossed them into their bin. And over all, the shrieking rasp of a file. The place smelled of hot pitch, and of the tallow that Leifsi, the younger apprentice, was stirring into a potful of it.

Today she could think only that her mother would clutch her headrail over her nose, exclaim at the din, and escape as soon as possible.

Leifsi turned, still stirring, to smile at her, and saw the basket. "God's mercy! Look what Jilly's brought us!" he cried with a cheerfulness that today grated on her like the sound of the file. "I beg you, put some in my mouth till I can leave this devil's brew—"

The noise abated as Toli and two fellow silversmiths ceased their work and glanced up from their shaping stakes.

"So spring is here at last," said Toli. He put down his hammer, left the handsome circular brooch he was embossing, and came forward, smiling. He was a twisted troll of a little man, muscled like an ox in spite of a hunched shoulder, and as good-humored as his wife was not. "Clever maid, to find a patch so quickly!"

"It is my brother has the sharp eyes," Juliana murmured, handing him the basket and turning to leave. She was in no mood for friendly exchanges. She had to wait for Leifsi, who was in her way, to pour the pitch into its little iron bowl, tilt the bowl this way and that to mound the viscous stuff toward the center, and set it aside, before she could edge past him.

"Will you have some porridge?" He teased her, gesturing toward the pitch-bowl as she moved past him. She liked Leifsi, who was near her own age. Usually he made her laugh and reminded her of Sweyn—the old, lighthearted Sweyn, as he had been in the old, lighthearted days. Today she wanted only to be alone.

She left them gathered eagerly around the basket, and went back through the earthy storeroom to the larger room behind, where Toli and Audrey and little Edana lived and slept and cooked and ate. A slightly crooked ladder led upward from one corner to the small three-sided loft. It was open on the ladder side, allowing the heat from the fire-pit to rise unhindered, and when the wind blew the wrong way over the hole in the thatch, it was smoky and occasionally uninhabitable; but it was usually warmer than the room below. There was a trucklebed like Old Coleruna's, woven of rye-straw with a turned-up edge that kept out draughts, and a small box for her belongings—of which she had none save the candle-ends that lighted her up to bed. It was a great improvement over any way she had lived since the striped ships came, but it would doubtless make her mother weep. Perhaps it would make *her* weep also, if she let herself think much about the old days—or even about living here the rest of her life.

There was no gainsaying it, she could never bring her mother here, surely not with the aim of proving that she could live well enough on her own.

She threw off her mantle and headrail, tugged off her muddy boots and bent to the floor for a handful of strewing-rushes to wipe them clean, then instead lay down for a moment on her narrow bed, her mind full of the picture of her mother's near-forgotten face.

What will she do if she comes here? she thought. *Will she cry out at sight of us, laugh aloud, weep? Will she take me in her arms, then scold because I ran away to the shore and could not be found? Will she say I did wrong to bring Wulfric here, instead of to Winchester? Uncle Robert will say so. Certainly she will try to make me go home with her—to that new husband's home. But she could never make me do what I did not wish to, unless Nurse Editha came and helped her. Perhaps the new husband will help her . . . But I will not heed him. Ever! A Norman father I will not have. Rather this loft for the rest of my days . . . rather the nunnery . . .* No, not the nunnery—that, too, was wild talk, and she knew it. She wanted no abbess, either, to reorder her life. What she wanted was so simple—to stay in Canterbury, wind wool for the great hanging, and find her own life—to be something besides the daughter of her mother. It was a longing her mother —and the new baron husband—would never understand.

Juliana sat up abruptly and began to wipe off her boots —the straw-stuffed boots of Brighid's dead brother.

It is not true, she told herself. I will not believe it until I see her standing by his side.

Meanwhile she must go down the ladder again to help Audrey bake the loaves. It would soon be time to sup.

T W E L V E

MINDFUL OF HER PROMISE TO BROTHER CADWALLA, Juliana passed through the abbey gates next morning while the bell for prime was still ringing, and shortly afterwards was in the workroom picking at the threads of his crooked spear. He had left his needle for her, thrust into the linen. It was a good one, of bronze, and had the dawn been a bright one she could have made quick work of delicately teasing the stitches loose one by one, and drawing the thread out, without disturbing the solid laid-and-couched work of the horse's flank underneath. But the sky was overcast, and peer as she would, she worked more by feel than by sight, constantly catching a rust-red thread instead of the dark brown one she was after, growing more tense by the moment for fear Brother Alain would come in and find her where she should not be, doing what she had not been told to do.

156

Slowly, though, the light brightened and the crooked stitches came loose, and she could thread the needle and set them in again, straight and true. She had barely finished when Brother Alain's brisk step sounded on the stairs. She stood up so suddenly that she overturned the stool, and was righting it, flushed and clumsy-fingered, when he entered. She retreated hastily to her place at the far end of the room, murmuring a greeting, not daring to look at him.

"Good morrow, child! You're here betimes."

"Yeh-so, Brother. I—I could not sleep longer. Will I wind the dark green first today?"

"Um. Yeh-so, the dark green. As well that as any."

His voice was preoccupied; she risked a glance and found him standing at Brother Cadwalla's place, a great roll of fine-woven linen slung over his shoulder. He was looking —she was sure—directly at the new-made spear. With her heart pounding guiltily, she drew in a breath, ready to defy him, to demand if he had fault to find with her stitches, to defend herself for only repaying kindness. Before she could speak, he did.

"What is your name, girl? Jilly?"

"Juliana!"

"Ah. Yeh-so. But I have heard them call you Jilly."

"Many do. Most do," she admitted. "I cannot stop them."

"You prefer your true name?"

"I do, then." She did not know why or when she had resolved to be Juliana to this monk. She knew only that she had.

"Then so I shall call you. Juliana, you embroider well. Those stitches are even and true."

She felt the heat rush up into her face, her hair. "As God hears me, I did not mean to—to do more than I ought. I meant only—"

"I know well what you were doing, and why you were doing it. Do not trouble yourself, child. I saw the kink in that spear yesterday and knew he would have no peace until it was straight again. A fine craftsman, Brother Cadwalla. He will set stitches here until he himself says 'ended.' But his eyes are going."

"I fear so, Brother."

"It is in God's hands." He moved to the long north side of the room and dropped his roll of linen under the high row of windows. Juliana turned to the hank of dark green, still warmed by his unexpected word of praise, and warming to him in spite of herself for the respect he paid Brother Cadwalla. In a moment the embroiderers began climbing the stairs to the workroom, and the day's work began.

Aside from a secret exchange of glances with her, Brother Cadwalla took no notice of the new-stitched spear, merely settled to his task as she settled to hers. But as she wound the dark green and then carded a brown fleece for the widow Godeleva's spinning, Juliana kept a curious eye on Brother Alain, who had summoned Brother Adam from his needle and set him to drilling tiny augur holes at intervals all along the north wall, at about head height. Into these Brother Alain was tapping a row of the thin, hard panelling pegs, burying them only halfway. And then together they stretched the new linen flat against the wall, hanging it to the pegs by the edge of the strip of coarser cloth sewn on all along the top. These extensions at top and bottom were twice as wide as the ones attached to the section on the frame. And the new section was only half as long as the one being worked on—the length of the room, no more.

Juliana was not the only close observer of the new activity. Old Widow Hildegarde and her pigeon-shaped daughter Elfgiva, whose stools were next to each other at the frame, had been murmuring together in their twittering voices and glancing as often at Brother Alain as at their work. The spinsters were openly watching, letting their hands mind their tasks. And half-deaf Christiana finally spoke out quite audibly to Brother Cadwalla.

"God's mercy, Brother, what are they doing? Are we to embroider the next length on the wall, then?"

Brother Alain's laugh rang out as he turned to face them all. "Even of such artists as you, I would not ask that. Indeed, I mean to make the work easier, for myself and you. This is the next length, yeh-so! I will draw the designs on it as it hangs here—not as it lies stretched on the floor of the refectory, which is a penance for a man's back! And I am having a different frame built. As you see, this section of linen is shorter than the first two, so there is no excess to roll up at the ends. And made wider with the extensions, so it may be rolled instead from top or bottom, as needed to bring every part in easy reach of your needles. We will complete the borders too, hereafter, instead of calling on the nuns. Those long pieces were too cumbersome! One must learn by doing, yeh-so? When a thing has not been done before!"

There was a murmur of comprehension and approval, laced with a few blunt comments from Christiana, who

159

remarked in her too-audible tones that t'was a pity it had not been thought of earlier. But Brother Alain only nodded his curly tonsure and heartily agreed with her, and Brother Adam, limping back to his work at the frame, paid no attention. It would be weeks, perhaps months, Juliana judged, before they finished the present section in any case.

At mid-morning, when the two monks returned from terce and Morrow Mass, Brother Alain was carrying a sheaf of parchment ends, plainly discards from the scriptorium, which he laid out in careful order on the floor beneath the new linen. Juliana, momentarily idle until Ingold finished a skein, edged close enough to see that they were covered with sketchings, swift, vigorous strokes of a charcoal stick, a few curves here barely indicating horses' rumps, a forked shape there saying "man," broad arches and peaks that meant "tower" or "hall" or "castle." And farther along came a series of lines with upcurved ends—the unmistakable profiles of ships.

That same afternoon, Brother Alain began to transfer his designs in full size upon the new linen. He worked with red chalk, lightly but with certainty, occasionally wiping out what did not please him, sometimes changing the position of a figure or the space between two. Juliana put her fingers in charge of her thread-winding and scarcely took her eyes off the pictures magically growing on the wall. Today her shoulders did not tire; she did not weary of the constant thin scraping of the wool against her fingers. She scarcely heard Christiana's sudden blurtings, Brother Cadwalla's soft replies, the twittering gossip of Widow Hildegarde and her daughter, the even pacings of the spinsters as they crossed and recrossed in front of her. She merely

160

watched and marveled, wishing powerfully that Wulfric could be here beside her, watching too.

One eventide in the second week of March, buying eels in Mercery Lane on her way home from the workshop, Juliana heard a familiar imperious voice, and turned to peer at a young woman standing at the ale-wife's stall. It was Averil, Lady Edwina's older daughter.

"Averil!" she gasped, and the other turned and stared at her.

"Jilly? Is it you?"

"It is, certainly," said Juliana, clutching Averil's arm and drawing her aside from the press of sellers and buyers in the marketplace. "How is this? Is your mother here, then? Is Bernadette?"

"All of us. Since two days back."

"And you mean to stay?"

"We must. Grimulf came first from Rochester, and told some renters they must move—my mother owns three houses here. They are poor enough places, but—"

"You have come from Rochester?"

"And before, from Otford," said Averil bitterly. "And before that from Lewes. All gone. We have not a hide of land left. Not one sheep of all those thousands. Four horses out of four-score . . . and these three houses. They have taken everything except my mother's bride-gifts."

No need to ask who "they" were. Lord Alfgar had owned large estates in Rochester, Otford, Lewes—all now in greedy Norman hands.

"Wulfric saw Grimulf a se'n-night ago—or thought he did. I did not believe him."

"Grimulf is all we have left. And Gytha—his wife, you remember, my mother's woman. And a groom and one of the housemaids. Though I daresay there are those worse off than we are," Averil added. Her prominent blue eyes widened as they examined Juliana more closely. "Jilly, is that your same old mantle and kirtle? Where are your shoes?" Apparently nothing would change Averil's high-born ways.

"I am one of those worse off than you," Juliana told her drily.

"But are you wed, then? You wear a headrail."

"I wear it for warmth. I am neither wed nor betrothed, nor likely to be!" Juliana glanced, suddenly conscious, at Averil's bare head. She was to have been wed last Christmastide.

"Aelfric is dead like my brothers," Averil said bleakly. "And poor Bernadette's betrothal was not yet signed . . . we have heard nothing since the ships came."

They were silent a moment. Then Juliana said, "Where is this house, Averil? I will find it. I must see your mother, and Bernadette."

"It is in Worthgate bertha, in Stour Street, at the corner where the lane turns to St. Mildred's. A stone house with a new thatch . . . come there with me now, Jilly. My mother will welcome you."

"Audrey must have these eels for the supper—I will come later. As soon as I can."

Conscious of the dusk fast gathering, Juliana sped back to Hethenmanne Lane, left the eels, and heedless of the meal she would be missing, hurried back along the lane and into Stour Street. She felt she could not wait to see

Lady Edwina—to fling herself into arms that would welcome her, that had known the old life, the old ways, that had embraced her mother, greeted her father.

She had no need to search for the house—Bernadette was standing before it, waiting, and flew to meet her the instant she appeared, to hug her and ply her with questions and urge her up the outside stair and into the house, which was a grander house than Juliana had stepped into for eighteen months, whatever Averil said. And in the far end of the room, where Lady Edwina waited, there was another greeting, as warm as she had hoped for, and indeed, watered with tears before it was finished.

"Juliana, my child! My lost Chelric's betrothed! My marriage-daughter-that-was-to-be! Alas, it will never be now, my Chelric is lost to us! Ah, God be merciful!" Lady Edwina hid her trembling mouth in a fold of her headrail, closed her eyes, and swayed back and forth.

"You have brought it all back to her," whispered Bernadette as Averil soothed her mother and called for Gytha to bring a draught of All-Heal herbs, laced with honey. "Usually she is able to forget that Chelric is dead—and our brother Hereward, and Father."

"Able to *forget*?" Juliana glanced at Lady Edwina in consternation. Certainly, she had changed from the stately and self-assured noblewoman in Juliana's memory. She looked older, and far thinner, her highbred features pale against her dark headcloth, her sunken eyes dimmer. "But—does she wish to?"

"I think she must. Too much has happened to us, too fast, Jilly. It is better when she can put it from her mind."

Or pretend to, so that she may turn a calm face to her

163

daughters, thought Juliana. Her gaze shifted to Bernadette. She too, had changed, thinned, grown taller—no longer the chattering nine-year-old who had been frightened by the long-haired star. She was now a quiet, soft-voiced maid with great hazel eyes, near the same age Juliana had been, herself, on the day the striped ships came.

"She will be calmer soon," said Averil, leaving her mother to Gytha's ministrations and coming back to her stool beside Juliana. "Do not ask about Rochester—about anything, Jilly," she said in a low voice. "Rather tell us of your family. Wulfric, too, is here? And your mother and Ragni? And Sweyn—?"

Dropping her own voice, Juliana told briefly the story of the months since they had met, her journey with Wulfric, something of their new lives here. Of her mother, she said only that she was safe in Winchester.

"With your uncle, yeh-so, I suppose it could not be helped," Averil said in disapproving tones. "He was always good to her . . . but I would he were not Norman!"

"I, also," Juliana said colorlessly.

"Say nothing of Normans to our mother, it will only distress her," Averil murmured as Gytha went back to tend the soup-kettle at the other end of the room, and Lady Edwina turned her chair and her attention to the three of them. Dry-eyed now and reaching for her finger-netting with hands only slightly trembling, she began talking as though she had last seen Juliana only a fortnight or two ago.

"Do you say you are working again at your embroidery? Ah, thread girl. At the abbey! Then it is an altar cloth you

164

make. A hanging? A large one! Indeed, so! For a bishop, is it?"

"I believe so, Lady," Juliana answered hurriedly. "I have been told it will hang in a church. I have—forgot—the name."

"Yeh-so, you were ever a forgetful child. But a good child, certainly. Daughters, tell Gytha that Juliana will sup with us this evening—Lenten fare only, but so it must be. Is your mother well, my love?"

"I hope so, Lady," murmured Juliana, as Averil, with a warning glance, went to do as she was bade.

It was a difficult conversation. But Juliana quickly became deft at forestalling the wrong questions or evading direct answers. And it was not long before Lady Edwina's hands steadied on her netting-work, the right one plying the long needle, the left fingers flying as of old in the complicated looping and holding and knotting as she fashioned a glove. At the same time her questions gradually gave way to the old stream of placid complaints about lazy servants, the wind, the cold, her daughters' carelessness —all addressed to no one in particular.

"It is better so," whispered Bernadette again, with a look, defensive, yet apologetic, in her hazel eyes. "Tell us more of your own life, Jilly. She will pay no heed."

So Juliana—somewhat defensive herself—explained about her attic at Toli's, and Brighid's dead brother's shoes, and the three pennies a month. "It is not—the old life. But it is a free one."

"It is not a proper life for your father's daughter," Averil objected. "You would do better to live here with us."

165

"My thanks, but I do very well at Toli's!" retorted Juliana, rebelling as always against Averil's overbearing ways. "I have had enough of alms!"

"It would scarce be alms," Bernadette put in quickly. "Averil, can you not learn to put honey on your tongue?"

"Nonsense—I did not mean . . ." Averil glanced at Lady Edwina's serene face and added bitterly, "Do not tell her you are not safe in your mother's home."

"As you will be, doubtless, the moment your mother learns where you are." Bernadette sighed. "God forgive me, Jilly, but I would you could stay here in Canterbury —even in your attic—now we are here."

"I wish it too! But—it may not be possible."

"Well, so. Life is as God wills it," Averil said bleakly. "I would I could *leave* Canterbury, and become a nun of St. Anastasia, which I longed for as a child. With Aelfric dead, what is there for me, else? But few get their wishes—and no Saxons, in this Norman world. Jilly will go to her mother, and I stay here with mine . . . You must not mind my saying so, Jilly, but I do not think your mother will recognize you in those rags you wear. Have you truly no others?"

"I do, certainly!" Juliana exclaimed—the more quickly because the same thought had been in her mind. "At least, I will. I mean to give one of my pennies next month for some of Audrey's weaving, to make a new kirtle—as best I can."

"You were never a seamstress! You must take one of mine," Averil told her. "And my old green mantle. Yeh-so, there is no cause to prattle about alms! I have never liked green with my complexion. You will do better to give the cobbler your penny for sounder shoes."

"She speaks truth, Jilly," Bernadette said softly. "Please take them, or we shall both feel hurt."

"I will, then. I thank you," said Juliana with difficulty and a sudden knot in her throat.

"You are freely welcome. You would have been our marriage-sister, remember, if life had been otherwise, and Chelric would have given you far more than a few old garments." Averil would not have been Averil had she not added, "We would be shamed to have you looking like a beggar-maid, when you are almost kin to us."

Bernadette caught Juliana's eye and rolled her own expressively upwards, in the old, droll way, and Juliana, stifling a sudden laugh, ceased thinking of her mother. Soon Gytha brought the food and Grimulf two beeswax candles, and for the space of an hour or two it seemed almost as though time had sped backwards, and the striped ships never been.

But the seeming went no deeper than the surface. As the days of Lent passed—busily for Juliana at the workroom and Wulfric at his books, emptily for the uprooted family of Lord Alfgar—Bernadette reported what Juliana could see for herself on her visits to the house on Stour Street: the life in Canterbury was not a good one for Lady Edwina.

"It is the idleness," Juliana told Wulfric as they walked one day at vespers toward Iron Bar Lane. "What can she do, that she once did? She has no great household to order, no flock of maidservants to keep busy, no fleeces always waiting to be carded and spun. She paces that little house all day, and mourns what is lost—or nets gloves and stockings, while the others try to help her forget her sons are dead."

"God pity the poor lady," Wulfric said in a subdued voice. He glanced thoughtfully at Juliana, and added, "I would not want to forget what *is*. Bad though it might be."

"Nor I," Juliana agreed slowly, wondering if she meant it. "But I am glad I have no time to brood." After a moment she added, "Bernadette wishes me to ask Brother Alain if her mother can join us in the workroom. But how can I do that? I am only the thread girl."

She was not long to remain so. One day in the week before Palm Sunday, Brother Cadwalla, frailer than ever these dark days of Lenten fasting and chill wind, took to his bed with an aching rheum, and soon sent word to Brother Adam that though he was better, his eyes were weary of straining and he would not return to the workroom. This surprised no one, but it posed a problem for Brother Adam, who in this season knew of no monk with the skill or the hours free of other duties to replace him.

"He suggests," Brother Adam told Juliana that morning, "that his young friend and helper Jilly take his needle. Do you think you can use it well enough to continue his stitching?"

Her breath catching in her throat, Juliana said, "As God hears me, I will try!"

"But who will then be thread girl?" demanded Christiana. "Already we wait for the thread to be spun. Now must we also wind it ourselves?"

"It is easier to find a thread girl than an embroiderer,"

Brother Adam pointed out. "Perhaps one of you knows some idle maid—or a needy woman—"

Before she could take thought, Juliana said swiftly, "I know such a maid, Brother. She is the daughter of a king's thane, one I knew at home, in Pevensey, lately come to Canterbury. She could wind your thread . . . I know her well, she was ever a friend to me, serious and trusty . . ." Breathless at her own daring, she added recklessly. "And her lady mother, if you should want her, is a fine spinster, one to match Widow Godeleva's speed and skill."

Brother Adam's eyes held a spark of surprised amusement under their thornbush eyebrows as he turned to examine her, but he said only, "Would she wish to spin for us? A great thane's lady?"

"The thane is dead, Brother, and Normans hold his lands. I—I think she would welcome it."

"Your friends have a friend in you." Brother Adam thought for a moment, then nodded. "Ask them, child. If they are willing, it could serve us well. Meanwhile, take Brother Cadwalla's needle and let us see how you go on."

He limped away to examine the rest of the work before settling on his stool. With fingers slightly unsteady from the speed at which things had changed in the past few minutes, Juliana threaded her needle and began to work. Though she knew herself to have been well and rigorously taught by Lady Edwina, it was nervous work at first, and slow because of the rigid care she was taking to make each stitch perfect, and ruthlessly pick out whatever was not. But as the morning wore on, her hands lost their clumsiness, and when Brother Adam began to read to them of

169

the life of St. Dunstan as he waited for thread, she forgot her fingers and began to use them with her accustomed ease. She was relieved but not really surprised when Brother Adam examined her work at midday and without comment merely smiled at her and left for sext.

It was the next morning, when she arrived early, eager to begin, that she found Brother Alain already there and working with his chalks. He was drawing the last scenes of the third section and had pegged up the blank linen of the fourth section above it on the wall. He turned at once to greet her, and told her that he could scarcely tell where Brother Cadwalla's work left off and hers began.

"Your hand is different, as every embroiderer's is different from every other's. But go on as you have begun, and the hanging will not suffer." He smiled, nodded away her stammered thanks—she was by now too much in awe of him to speak naturally in his presence. Then he added, "Brother Adam has told me of your friends from Pevensey."

"Oh. Yeh-so. I have asked them, Brother, and they will come tomorrow—or it may be Monday—to join us. I will bring them. Today Lady Edwina was not—not quite well . . ." In truth, yesterday having been the birthdate of her firstborn, Hereward, Lady Edwina had wept for him all morning and gone to pray in church all afternoon, and Averil had decreed that she must rest in her bed until she grew calmer. Juliana could only hope the new work itself would calm her, so that such days would not come often.

Brother Alain merely waved the apology aside, repeating, with an odd intentness in his bright blue eyes, "From Pevensey. You come from Pevensey too, then?"

170

"It was my birthplace, and my home. Until—" She broke off, swallowing.

"Until?"

"Until the—ships came."

"You were there? That very morning—Michaelmas Eve? You saw the ships?"

"I did. I—was at the shore. There was fog . . ." Her throat closed.

"It is hard for you to speak of it."

"It is, then." Images of the old dream rose like phantoms.

Brother Alain came toward her, looked carefully into her face. "I do not wish to cause you pain, Juliana. But if you could speak of it—" He broke off, gestured toward the work on the frames, the chalked-in new section on the wall. "I am trying to draw a truthful tale. This work was begun by Norman command; it will hang in a great Norman church. But it must not tell only a Norman truth."

"I understand," she breathed. The old suspicions were dissolving in her mind like mist. It was as if she had willed him to say this.

"So I have taken great care with this," he went on. "I have spoken to Saxons who were with Earl Harold in Normandy. I myself saw King Edward buried in his new abbey at Westminster. I have questioned villagers who watched the great battle at Caldbec Hill, and a Saxon archer who survived it. But I have found no one from Pevensey—until today."

After a difficult moment, Juliana said again, "I understand, Brother. I will speak of it. I will try."

Footsteps sounded on the stair. Brother Alain's glance

171

flashed to the doorway, returned, bright with thanks, to her face. "No need to do this now. But Sunday? After all the processions and the mass. I will come here and wait for you."

Widow Hildegarde and Elfgiva, softly twittering together as always, came into the workroom, and Brother Alain turned away. Juliana, dry-mouthed and wondering if she could indeed do what she had promised, went to her stool and took up her needle.

T H I R T E E N

PALM SUNDAY, TWO DAYS LATER, DAWNED CLEAR AND
springlike—the first day the sky had shone pale blue, the
sun hinted at warmth. Before first light Juliana and Bernadette, with Toli's two apprentices—and little Edana, carried good-naturedly on Goldwin's broad shoulders—were
already in the woodlands northwest of Canterbury. They
had passed through Westgate as matins rang through the
darkness, in company with half the other young people of
the town. Those who had not scattered through the woods
near Blean had gone northeast or southwest, through other
gates, to find the early-flowering willow they all called English Palm. Before full sunup Leifsi discovered a fine stand
of it along a little hillside creek, and Juliana, flushed and
pleasantly tired from the hour's walk, busily cutting the
leafy fronds with Audrey's second-best knife, was almost
able to forget the promise made to Brother Alain, and the
conversation coming this day after mass.

It will not be hard to speak of it once I begin, she told herself firmly—as she had been telling herself at intervals throughout the last two days. And I need not begin for a few hours yet—*so do not think of it.*

"Jilly, I cannot reach those—see, the fine ones up there! Come with your long arms and legs—"

Juliana dropped her armful onto the growing pile and went to help Bernadette, shaking out the folds of Averil's old green mantle—now her new one. Under it was Averil's old white kirtle and scarlet *rocc,* neither one chafing her armpits nor riding up over her wrists, but full and easy. Their ample folds were cinched to her slimmer figure by her own old girdle, and under all was a linen undertunic, fresh and new. As for the sound new shoes—cobbled to fit her feet, not Brighid's dead brother's—they made her feel she walked on air. It was joy enough to sweep from her mind all uneasy thoughts of the promise she must keep.

As the sun rose the five of them were sitting on the gentle slope of the hillside, catkins twined in their hair or stuck behind their ears, fashioning small talisman crosses as they watched the light grow, calling greetings to other searchers who trooped past. The sky was the color of roses, brightening to flame.

"We always used to go up to that woodland above our horse pastures, do you remember, Jilly?" Bernadette said dreamily.

"I do, certainly."

"And Sweyn carried Ragni just as Goldwin has carried Edana, and Wulfric was forever putting catkins down our necks . . ."

Juliana glanced at little Edana, sitting primly now on a cushion of dry bracken Goldwin had cut for her, her thin little fingers fumbling with her willow fronds under Bernadette's guidance. Ragni was just such an age when Juliana had seen her last—only three or four years old. By now she would be no longer a toddler but a little maid, all legs, no doubt, like one of the new spring fillies. And their mother? Would she still be herself, or changed like Lady Edwina? Juliana scarcely dared think of it, yet questions hovered like shadows around every day that passed. The answers would come soon enough.

Do not think of that, either, she ordered herself sternly.

"What, not finished? And I thought you would work much faster than an oaf like me," Leifsi teased her as he set his first little cross aside and got up, stretching.

"Not I! I can never bind the center of the arms to suit me."

"Let me help you."

Leifsi hunkered down beside her, examined the binding and began to pull it tighter, taking the willows from her hands without a by-your-leave and as usual reminding her of Sweyn, who had always found fault with the binding of her crosses and insisted on fixing them for her. Everything was reminding her of bygone times this morning. No marvel in that; each Palm Sunday since she could remember— save only last year—she had gone out before dawn into the woodlands, and every move, every familiar sight and sound and birdsong carried echoes of other years. Last year alone, spitting fowl and emptying slops at the fortress in Hastings, she had made no cross to keep through the twelvemonth for good luck. Good luck had come anyhow, by God's mercy—or Wulfric's stubbornness.

"You say little this morning," Leifsi remarked with one of his quick, half-shy glances at her from under his dark forelock as he handed back her cross. His manner ever veered between shy and brazen, impertinent and abashed, in a way that left her uncertain of his true nature. She suspected he was uncertain of it himself. "But then, you seldom do," he added. "You are never a scold like Audrey, God be thanked!"

"Am I so silent, then?"

"You are no chatterbox. I often wonder what you are thinking."

"Why not ask? I was thinking of my brother."

"The one who studies with the scriptors?"

"Him, too, yeh-so. He is out here this morning somewhere, with the other schoolboys. But I have an older brother . . ." Her voice trailed off.

"And where is he, then?"

After a moment she said, "I do not know."

He studied her face briefly, his greenish eyes speculative, then plucked some new willows from the pile and began to fashion another cross. "I have brothers," he said carelessly. "I know where they are, all too well! One is at home in Littlebourne, in my father's smithy, complaining that I am not there too. The other is 'prenticed to the miller at Westgate. In easy reach to come begging of me!" He shot her a quick glance and added, "Like me, he wearied of making plows, and kettles for the village wives, and pounding iron all day."

He was telling her plainly that he came from humble folk, and was trying to better himself. He was an odd youth, but likeable.

"And do you find silver work better?"

"One cannot compare them—silver with iron!" His voice had lost its flippant tone, become serious and respectful. "I have always wanted to fashion such things as Toli makes. But I am fearful slow in learning—Goldwin is already doing embossed work, while I still pour pitch. And burn myself," he added ruefully with a rub at the red scar on one hand.

"Goldwin has been 'prenticed longer. No doubt last year he, too, poured pitch." Juliana reached for willows and began on a second cross. She had promised to bring one for Averil, who would not come out with them, saying such things were for the young, and someone must look to the household. Averil was not twenty, but the death of her betrothed—all that had happened—seemed to have convinced her that her life was over. *Well, so, mine is not, then!* Juliana told herself, tugging vigorously on the new binding. *I will have one, Normans or no.*

It occurred to her that Leifsi's life, like the plowman Oswig's of whom Wulfric had told her, like Toli's, seemed not much altered from what it was before the ships came.

"Did the Normans come to Littlebourne?" she asked him curiously.

"The Normans came everywhere, did they not?"

"But—did they not destroy it?"

Leifsi shrugged. "Who would destroy a smithy? Normans need horseshoes and buckles, and lances mended, like other folk."

It was as she had thought. A change of masters—that was all.

After a moment Leifsi added quietly, "They burned the thane's hall and took his lands. A Norman knight collects the rents at quarter-day now. As in your town of Pevensey. Where your father was thane." As she looked up swiftly, he said, "Your friend, the maid Bernadette, told me of him."

"I do not want to talk of it."

"We will not, then," he said at once. "Shall I tighten that binding for you?"

"It is finished." Juliana showed him the second cross, picked up the first one, and got to her feet, tucking both crosses into the pocket of her kirtle. Leifsi scrambled to his feet, too, but she left him and joined Bernadette, who was setting off with Goldwin to cut more of the longer willows they would carry in the processions. A full circuit of the city walls they would walk, behind the abbot and the Brothers, and through the streets of the town, and around the nave of St. Peter and Paul in the abbey before mass.

Talk of Pevensey and her father she must—with Brother Alain. After mass. Until then she wished only to savor this happy morning.

At midmorning, as the mass-goers dispersed from St. Peter and Paul, Juliana dropped her palm-frond onto the stack outside the nave doorway and walked on dragging feet toward the workroom.

It is foolish, she told herself, to think I cannot talk of a thing, just because I never have. Yet she felt as if she were about to open a coffer best left tight closed. For no one save Brother Alain would she have done it.

Clutching the little palm cross in her pocket, she mounted the stone stair, forcing briskness into her step. Soonest begun, soonest ended.

He was there ahead of her, his curly black tonsure bent over a drift of sketches spread on the table, his hands moving swiftly among them, choosing, discarding. The vivid blue eyes flashed her a glance of welcome.

"God's blessing on you, child, on this fine holy day! I hope I do not ask too painful a task of you? I would not do so for a lesser reason. You understand?"

"Yeh-so, Brother." Juliana's gaze flew anxiously to the sketches, but they were a maze to her, a weaving of bold dark lines. She could not focus calmly enough to make sense of them.

In any case, Brother Alain stepped in front of them. "Do not look at these yet, they are incomplete. I know nothing of the landing at Pevensey—save that the ships landed, that the town was subdued, that a feast of victory was prepared for Duke William and his nobles, and that a castle of sorts was raised within a few days and most of the men moved on to Hastings. So much my patron has told me. It is a Norman view."

It was, certainly. It was unrecognizable. A feast? A castle? Juliana's mind touched gingerly upon her memories, found animals seized and slaughtered—perhaps for the roasting spits—and before that, Normans carrying planks and tools from the boats, coming toward her, straight up the path to

179

the old Roman fort where she stood watching . . . The old panic stirred, and her thoughts swerved hastily.

"My need is for Saxon details." Brother Alain was moving with his springy step toward the pegged-up linen of sections three and four on the wall, both now fully chalked in. "Look at this, first, Juliana. Come, let us begin at the start of it, and I will explain as we go."

Willingly she followed him, her eye captured at once by the strength and pattern of his drawings. The once-blank linen was lively now with figures and castles and movement, the scenes flowing easily from one into the next by means of a gesturing hand or a turning head.

"At the time of these scenes, Earl Harold has already returned from Normandy," said Brother Alain. "And King Edward has finished his new abbey at Westminster—consecrated, alas, on the day before his death. Now. Here is King Edward on his deathbed, with his queen mourning at his feet, and his servant and a priest supporting him. This figure beside him is Earl Harold—and do you see, the king's hands stretch out to him, to touch his. He is bequeathing him the kingdom."

"Oh, he did so, certainly!" breathed Juliana, her spirits lifting a little. "There can be no doubt of it! My father said so!"

"No, there is no doubt of that. And here, in the next scene, they are telling Earl Harold the king is dead, and offering him the crown. And here—here is Harold crowned and enthroned, with the nobles offering fealty on one side, and Archbishop Stigand on the other . . ."

Stigand! Juliana could still hear the deaf old hermit's

disgusted voice: *A man excommunicated by five popes!* She said swiftly, "Harold was not crowned by Archbishop Stigand, Brother, but by Ealdred of York! I know this. My father—"

"Yeh-so, yeh-so, I know it too, child. Does my drawing show Stigand setting the crown on his head? Do my words, above there, say he did so?"

"I—I cannot read the words."

"They merely tell who he is. You must understand that Bishop Odo, who has ordered this hanging, wishes certain prominent people to appear on it. I must bow to such commands—wherever they do not change the truth."

Juliana searched his calm face and said nothing. *The world is as it is.* But as he moved on to the next scene, her glance lingered mutinously on the figure of the discredited Stigand—to whom not even bishops came for consecration. Change the truth it might not, but what *appeared* was that he had just placed the crown on Harold's head. As Odo doubtless wished it to appear.

Brother Alain was already explaining the pointing courtiers who came next—the long-tailed star they were pointing at—the word of it being brought to Harold on his throne. "For it was plainly an omen of great import. The oath of Bayeux had been broken—"

Juliana's attention switched abruptly from the drawings. "The oath? You—you believe he swore that oath? You have put it in the drawings?"

"I have, certainly. It comes near the end of the second section there on the frame, ahead of where your needles are working—we have not yet unrolled those final scenes.

181

It is not a matter of believing, child—the truth of the oath is not in question."

After a moment Juliana spoke stiffly, around the knot in her throat. "That, too, is a Norman view."

Brother Alain looked at her curiously, but seriously. She met his eyes, her heartbeat slow and heavy. "Juliana, there were many witnesses. I have talked to men—Saxon and Norman—who were there in William's castle in Bayeux, watching. Two reliquaries were brought into the hall—they held old and sacred relics. And Harold stretched out both hands and touched them, and made his oath."

It was the same as Sweyn had told it—the two boxes, the touching with both hands, the swearing before many witnesses. So it was, then. The truth of the oath was not in question.

"But what did he swear to, Brother Alain?" Juliana realized she was pleading, begging. "Fealty to William in Bayeux—yeh-so! But not in England!"

"Fealty is not an oath of place, child, but of condition. Were not Harold's men his men in Normandy, as well as at home? Likewise William's were his in England—Harold, too."

"But Earl Harold—as God hears me, I cannot believe Earl Harold Godwinson swore an oath—then broke it! He would not do so base a thing, a man like that—my father loved him till his death! It must be a lie, a Norman lie!" Juliana choked off her outburst, gasped, "I crave pardon, Brother, I should not speak so to you . . ."

"Juliana, sit here a moment. Let us talk of this." Brother Alain pulled a stool out from the frame, perched himself

182

on the table nearby. "You had a high regard for Harold Godwinson—that is plain."

"I did, then! I do still! Not I alone, my father—he was King Harold's man in all his battles, until he fell beside him! Indeed, there were many such—hundreds!"

"Not hundreds but thousands so staked their lives and fortunes on him. He was a great hero. A man above baseness—you are right."

"Then, how—"

"But still he was a man, Juliana, not a demigod or saint—nor yet a martyr."

"I . . . yeh-so. A noble man!"

"A noble man caught in a trap no man could open—in William's country, in William's power, in William's debt for rescue and for honors heaped upon him. What could he do, when asked for an oath, but swear it?"

Juliana's lips parted to fling back an answer—but she could find none.

"And what could he do," Brother Alain went on gently, "when King Edward and the *witan* bade him rule England, but break the oath he had sworn, and take the crown?"

Juliana stared at her hands in silence. *What could he do, else?* Sweyn had said. And indeed, indeed, the answer was "nothing." The man Harold was a man—a bold leader but not a demigod, not a saint, not the fabled hero she had half-worshiped all her life—and a martyr was not what England needed. The crown had been his, by command of king and *witan*—but not his to give to William, whatever he had sworn to. The trap was fast shut on him. "I had not thought of it that way," she whispered.

183

"Think of it, then. It is easy to blame great ones for their missteps—when we know nothing of their dilemmas. It is Christian to forgive."

I would never blame him, she thought. But she wondered if she could ever be Christian enough to forgive the exchange of great hero for—plain man. It was as if Harold Godwinson were newly dead, this time for always. She said only, "Yeh-so, Brother. I will try." She sucked in a long breath. "Let us—let us look at the drawings."

He got up at once, and led the way back to the pegged-up linens. "Now—where did we leave off? Here—at the long-tailed star, and the nobles bringing word of it to Harold. And in the border below—do you see?" The intensity, the excitement was coming back to his voice. "I have drawn just the hint of ships on the water, a line-sketch only, to suggest what is to come. For there can be no doubt of what the omen foretold."

No doubt at all. Juliana kept silence, struggling to put the oath and Harold from her mind and to ignore the hollowness inside her. Slowly, caught up in spite of herself by the vigor of his telling, she stepped with Brother Alain along the chalked linen as the story unfolded—the news of Harold's crowning carried to Normandy by William's spies, William ordering a fleet made ready; fierce, relentless preparations as trees were felled, planks cut, ships built and set afloat. Here section four of the linen began, with weapons and armor and food and kegs of wine all carried to the shore to be loaded, and knights riding their great stallions to go aboard. And then the beast-headed ships were abroad on the swelling waves, one after another, a great crowd of

184

them, with their striped sails taut, shields glinting in rows along the gunwales, and all the dark heads clustered behind . . . Juliana's breath caught and for a moment the room blurred through a hot rush of tears. Quickly she blinked them away.

"It was just so, Brother—just so they came out of the fog, one after another—scores of them—with all their men and horses. I had been playing by myself on the shore . . ."

"You saw them landing?"

"I did, then." She was seeing them again as she stared at the stretch of empty linen still waiting for the chalk. "I could not believe they were real ships—then I could not move for fear. They drove the prows deep into the pebbles—the horses were struggling and frightened, but they did not heed that, they made them jump into the shallows . . ."

"Did they not see you, child?"

"It may be—but I ran. There is a Roman fortress—a ruin only—there on the higher ground, and I climbed over a broken place in the wall. I watched from there . . . I could not look away, but then they came climbing after me up the path, bearing tools and planks—"

"It was no doubt there they made their fortifications."

"No doubt. I did not wait to see." Her throat was closing again. She turned away quickly from the chalked ships, the still-blank linen with its frightening visions, and found that Brother Alain was choosing sketches from the scattering on the table.

"Here—I have armored horsemen starting into the town—"

"Yeh-so—" She swallowed hard, tried again. "Yeh-so, certainly, many of them mounted at once, and they were armed, but they did not put their helmets on, because there was no guard to stop them. Not one challenger! All the *fyrd* had gone home to their harvests. There was only I . . . and I ran and ran, shouting for my father, but he could never have heard me, and I kept stumbling and could not get my breath. And when I got to the market square at last it was full of Normans—and the village wives fleeing from the horses' hooves—and blood . . . And oh, God help me, I cannot tell any more!"

Brother Alain was already turning her away from the sketches toward the windows, telling her with dismay in his voice that she need speak no more, not one word, saying in remorse that he should never have asked it. She barely heard him. She was back in the square, with Alflaed the harbormaster lying slaughtered like the harvest-feast cow, and Rhonwen screaming and screaming. And she found she could not stop now.

"A horseman grabbed me," she heard herself saying, in a low and trembling voice. And then she was telling the rest of it, all of it—more than she had ever told Wulfric, far more than she had told Sweyn. Even from the old terrible dream she had always waked herself with her stifled cries of "Father! Normans!" and stopped short of Jutta's blood and the burning hall and those wraithlike children appearing through the rushes, and the measureless time of sitting in Grim the salter's little hut—and the battlefield red and cluttered, humming with flies. Now she could not stop; she told it all.

When it was finished she found herself standing rigid by

the window, staring out at the road that lay alongside the gate below. An old man appeared around the curve of the abbey wall, leading a donkey. With an effort she focused on him; became gradually aware of the balmy air of this first spring midday on her face. She swallowed, and found the knot gone. Slowly her shoulders began to ease.

Behind her, Brother Alain's firm voice said, "It is over now, Juliana. It is in the past."

"I—I would I could make it stay there."

"Perhaps you will, now. It is sometimes good to speak of—what is too hard to speak of."

She nodded, dimly grasping that he meant to comfort her. After a moment she walked slowly back to the table, looked at the jumble of sketches, drew one toward her, then another. "Truly, you needed me to speak of it. Here are Normans, the houses of a town. But where is the harvest-feast cow? My father's burning hall?"

"As God hears me, they will be there, Juliana, on the linen. You have my oath on it. The slaughtered animals, your mother and brother fleeing. I will forget nothing you have said." Brother Alain paused, then added gently, "I will draw your memories on the linen. Try to leave them there, pinned fast with embroidery. Change them into thread."

Juliana looked at him, her eyes filling. "Thank you, Brother. I will try."

Into the silence came the brazen clang of the abbey bell, ringing for sext and High Mass. Brother Alain stirred, and began to shuffle his sketches together; Juliana turned to go. He stopped her with a light touch on her arm.

"As for that other oath we spoke of, child—the broken

187

one—no man can unsay it now. But think well on what we said here. It may ease the soreness in you to make your peace with truth. To be angry with it is folly. To deny it has never changed it yet."

"I understand." Juliana swallowed painfully, and said again, "I will try."

F O U R T E E N

GOOD FRIDAY CAME, AND CREPT BY LIKE ALL GOOD FRI-
days, with no familiar ringing of terce and sext and nones
to mark the hours, but only the constant dismal tolling of
the abbey bell; the spirit flagged, the silver-shop was silent,
the embroidery workshop empty, the church stripped of
all ornament but yew boughs, the mass long and somber,
and it seemed to Juliana the day would never end. In the
hour before dusk, silent and idle on her straw bed in the
loft while Toli's family and apprentices sat silent and idle
below, Juliana heard a knock at the back door and Toli's
voice. A moment later Leifsi appeared at the foot of her
ladder, saying, "Your brother is asking for you."

Surprised and puzzled, she hurried down to find Wulfric
still standing by the door, though Toli was hospitably offering a place on the apprentices' bench.

"Come with me awhile, please, Jilly," he said with a quick
smile, and turned away at once.

189

"Come where? Why are you not at your dorter? Brother Odbold—"

Wulfric said only, "It will not take long," and was out the door before she could protest further.

She caught up with him a few paces down Hethenmanne Lane. He was not heading for the center of town but toward the river and King's Bridge. "Wulf, where are we going? In God's name, will you not—"

"We are going to see someone. Not Mother—it is not Mother, you needn't think that. It is—Beorc."

He had dropped his voice so low that she was not certain she had heard him. "Beorc?"

"Hsst! Yeh-so, he who stole our mantles and herrings, the carpenter's son from Pevensey. Keep quiet, there are folk around."

There were few at this hour, on this day, but Juliana lowered her voice in spite of a sudden breathless excitement. "Is Sweyn with him, then? Where did he come from? What does he want?"

"He will tell you. Sweyn is not with him, though he sent him—first to find me at the school, and through me, you. Here, across the bridge now. Hold your tongue and hurry."

He had begun to set such a pace that she could do little but obey. They walked, half-running, to the end of St. Peter's Street and through Westgate into the more open countryside. Beyond the mill a lane turned off northward; they followed it for a furlong, slowed as they approached a cottar's clay-and-wattle hut set among a cluster of outbuildings. There Wulfric left the lane and picked his way across a new-plowed field to a stable farthest from the house. He gave a low whistle as he stepped inside. Juliana, at his heels, was met by the reek of horse and trampled straw, and saw a dim figure come through the gloom to meet them.

"Good even, Thane's Daughter. I thank you for coming."

"Sweyn—where is Sweyn? Why did you come here?"

"He is hurt, Thane's Daughter. He sent me—"

"Hurt? How? Is it—"

"Wounded. In one of our . . . battles. An arrow found him as we got away. We have tended him, but . . . it is a bad wound, feverish. He cannot ride, and the companions must move north the day after Easter, to join the Aetheling in York. There is a great gathering . . ."

"But what will he do? Wounded, and alone?"

"He says you will care for him and hide him—if you can—until he can follow us."

"I? But . . . Yeh-so, I will, as God hears me! I can, I must! Only I do not know . . ." Juliana's thoughts were spinning. *How* could she care for a wounded man in her attic? Audrey would never let him in the house . . . *Oh, God's mercy, Sweyn badly hurt, and feverish* . . . "I must think. I will do it. But I must think of a way . . . Where is he? Near?"

"Near enough. He is safe until Sunday. Find him a place, and I will bring him—on Easter Sunday, while all the world is in church—you, too, so you will not be missed. I promise no one will see or tell."

Wulfric spoke up. "But what of afterwards? When he is well?"

"Ah, when he is well he will have no trouble. He can

191

look exactly like a peddler—you will not know him yourself. If it were not for the wound . . . but peddlers should not have arrow wounds in their backs."

Juliana shivered, went hot and cold with imagining, and clenched her teeth, to keep them from chattering with anxiety. "I do not know where I will hide him. But I will do it, I take oath on it—tell him so. Come here tomorrow at this time. I will have something arranged."

"I will be here, Thane's Daughter. God b'with you."

Beorc stepped back into the shadows, and Wulfric tugged at her sleeve. They slipped outside into the gathering dusk, retraced their steps along the lane, and passed through Westgate before the gatekeeper barred it for the night. Once inside the walls, Wulfric slowed a bit.

"What will you do, then? *How* will you arrange it?"

"I told you! I do not know."

But she did. There was only one way she could arrange anything—and that was to speak to Lady Edwina. The house on Stour Street was a private house, a house of Saxons, a place of safety and sanctuary for Sweyn—provided Lady Edwina could bear the shock, provided the strain of sheltering him would not send her weeping and unnerved to pray in church all day, maybe too upset to spin in the workroom as usual, to keep a calm face for the weeks Sweyn might need to mend. Juliana's mind was ringing with remembered warnings: *Say nothing of Normans to our mother, do not ask about Rochester . . . do not tell her you are not safe in your mother's home . . .* How could one bring her sons' friend Sweyn to her with an arrow wound in his back? Juliana lay long awake that night, but found no answer.

Nevertheless, she rose with the sun next morning, dressed, and started at once for Stour Street. There would be no embroidering today; the monks would be busy with their vigils, with refurbishing the church, and in every house the women would be baking and cooking and polishing. Lines would form at the confessionals as Canterbury finished the long penitence of Lent and prepared soul and body for the joy of Easter.

Bernadette met her at the open doorway, having seen her hurrying toward the outside stair. "Jilly! I did not know if we would see you today, with nothing going forward at the workroom. Shall I have Gytha—bring bread . . . ?" Her voice turned anxious as she studied Juliana's face.

"I want no bread. I must speak to your mother." Juliana tried to school her features to blankness. There was no use attracting the attention of all the household—until it was needful. "I beg you, in private."

"Of course! I will send the servants away."

Easy enough to do that—the groom was already in the stables, Grimulf with him; Gytha and the housemaid were soon dismissed. But Averil was coming forward, ready to offer Juliana a stool near her mother's chair; Bernadette was there already. No sending them away.

They will have to know, soon or late, thought Juliana, sinking down on the stool with knees gone suddenly weak. All of them, servants too. What if one of them should betray Sweyn? She fixed her eyes on Lady Edwina, who looked calmly back at her.

"What is it, child? You are very pale."

"I must say something—I must ask something—that will distress you."

193

"Then do not ask it!" said Averil swiftly. "Jilly, we have told you—"

"Hsst, Averil, be silent," said her mother. And to Juliana she said, "Ask."

Juliana swallowed, tried to moisten her dry mouth, and blurted it out. "Lady, my brother Sweyn is wounded. He has been fighting Normans. He is ill and in danger. He needs a place to hide, and me to nurse him! Will you take us in?"

Bernadette gasped; Averil made a quick motion that was stilled by her mother's gesture. Lady Edwina sat silent a moment, straight and stiff in her chair, her hands clenched in her lap, her gaze fixed fiercely on Juliana's face. Then, "I will, certainly," she said in a voice like iron. Before Juliana could gather her wits enough to realize the hurdle was taken, the worst moment behind her, she added, "You had best tell me all of it."

With shaking voice and unsteady breath, Juliana told all she knew of what Sweyn had been doing, how he had lived since the battle of Caldbec Hill, told of Beorc's coming and what he had said. Lady Edwina listened without moving, without expression except that her eyes burned in her rigidly composed face. Juliana found herself thinking, *She was a king's thane's lady, after all. She is a warrior's widow.*

There was another silence when Juliana had finished. Even Averil said nothing, only watched her mother anxiously.

Still in that level voice, Lady Edwina said, "Tell Beorc to bring him here. And come, yourself. You should be

194

sharing my daughters' bed like the sister you were meant to be. Go back now and tell your moneyer that the family of your once-betrothed have made you take your rightful place in their house. No one will think the move strange. Grimulf shall arrange a bed for Sweyn in the lower store-room beside his own, and help with the nursing. No one in this household will speak of his presence; no one of us would speak to any Norman of anything at all. Grimulf shall not go to church on the morrow; when the rest of us return, Sweyn will be here, and safe. You will sleep here tomorrow night."

"I will, Lady," choked Juliana. "May God reward you."

"But my mother—" Averil began dazedly, and was silenced.

"I will do what is needful, Averil! Can you not see? It is a way to fight. Go, now, send Grimulf to me."

Juliana took one of the thin, tense hands, kissed it quickly, and left the house accompanied by Bernadette, whose eyes were wide with excitement. Averil followed, her thoughts plainly less on the problems ahead than on her mother.

"She is like her old self! But tomorrow—? Will she not forget Jilly is to sleep here, and be dismayed to see a wounded man in our storerooms?"

"She will not," said Bernadette. "She forgets only what is past changing."

"She need never think of Sweyn again, she need never see him! I will do everything!" Juliana promised. "But I fear Toli will think me ungrateful."

"Let me go with you!" exclaimed Bernadette. "I will tell

195

Leifsi how I begged you to come—and he will tell Toli, and Toli will tell Audrey—"

"Audrey! So long as I do not ask for my penny back, Audrey will be happy to see me go!"

That day and the next were strange ones, the hours now rushing by, now drawing out until it seemed time itself had stopped. From confession on Easter Saturday and throughout Easter Sunday, as she prayed diligently for Sweyn's health and took the communion wafer alongside Bernadette and waited the hours out in the flower-decked church, she could think of nothing but Beorc and his helpless companion, and how they would travel, and what might be happening on some woods road, or at a town gate, or in Lady Edwina's lower storeroom. It was a penance to walk sedately back to Stour Street beside Lady Edwina's pony, pretending to talk to Averil and Bernadette—who were only pretending too—when anxiety told her to run, to fly, to find out at once if all was well.

And all was well, though it was another painful quarter-hour before she could see it for herself. Her impulse to rush directly through the low arched doorway to the half-underground storerooms beneath the house was curbed by Lady Edwina's thin, firm fingers, which captured her shoulder and propelled her up the outside stair and into the upper living quarters as if it were any Sunday in the year. Belatedly mindful of the passing townspeople on their way home from church, Juliana waited, twisting her hands and pacing the long room, until Lady Edwina summoned Gytha to bring a pitcher and told Juliana to fetch ale from the storerooms for the Easter supping.

"Do not hurry. Walk calmly and stay only a few moments. You may go to him again after dark."

Schooling her movements to be casual, Juliana obeyed. Once in the earthy half-gloom of the storerooms, she groped her way past the half-empty shelves with their careful hoard of kegs and sacks and sealed jugs, through the homely smells of barley and bean-flour and beer and salt fish and onions, toward the gleam of a rushlight showing from a lower level. There, in the small room with the well and its buckets in one corner, she found a new straw pallet next to Grimulf's old one, and Sweyn upon it, tossing and rolling his tangled fair head, and Grimulf himself hunched over a basin like some ancient wizard, wetting a cloth and wringing it out in his big-knuckled hands.

She fell upon her knees at once, whispering,. "Sweyn, it is I! *Sweyn!*"

But Grimulf said gruffly, "He will not heed you, Thane's Daughter. He is out of his senses. If it please you—do you give me the cloth on his forehead, and spread this one there."

"Yeh-so, yeh-so, give it to me. Oh, God's mercy . . . how thin he looks!" She swallowed painfully. "Will he die?"

"He will not, then." Grimulf's brusque tone was as bracing as his matter-of-fact acceptance of wounds and fever, of which, Juliana thought, he had no doubt seen plenty in his years with Lord Alfgar. "He was ever a strong boy. He has had a bad journey, to come here, jolting about in an ironmonger's wagon. He will be better when the fever cools."

"But can we do nothing but wring out cloths?"

197

"Patience, Thane's Daughter. Gytha has the red oil of St. John's wort in plenty, and dried comfrey. She will make a poultice for his wound tomorrow, when I can turn him over."

"I will make the poultice! I will do everything—I wish he would not toss so!"

"He will ease presently. Wait for tomorrow. You had best take the ale-jug and go above now."

"I will come back—after dark. Then I will nurse him, and *you* may go."

"As you wish, Thane's Daughter." Grimulf's gray mustache tilted with a slight smile. "There will be nursing a-plenty for both of us, labor we ever so well. Go now, it is in God's hands."

So began a fortnight of a strange double life, in which all was as usual on the surface, everything different underneath. Calmly embroidering in the daytime, watching Brother Alain's sketchy lines take on color and texture and richness on the linen, watching Lady Edwina pace back and forth with the other spinsters, her spindle twirling, her hands flying, her eye critically ordering all the workshop, Juliana could hardly believe that at sunup she had helped Grimulf fight Sweyn into submission while they bathed him and changed the poultice on his ugly wound, that at vespers she would be back in the dim little well-room, doing it all again. The persistent fever made their nursling into a single-minded captive, determined to break free.

"He thinks he must up and ride north, you'll not talk him out of it," Grimulf told her when she tried to reason with Sweyn. "Best help me hold him till his strength gives out. He can't keep this up long."

Grimulf was right, as usual, but for some days Sweyn remained an unruly stranger, his own weakness their only ally. Finally, one twilit evening when she stole down to the storerooms dreading the usual struggle, she found him alone in the room, limp and passive, the glazed brightness gone from his eyes and intelligence there instead.

"Sweyn! You are better! God's mercy, the fever has gone!"

"Thanks to you, little sister—and Lord Alfgar's old servingman." His voice was a thread, but he smiled a little, the battle scar dragging down his eye in the way she remembered from the forest. "I could not believe who I was seeing, when I woke an hour ago and found him beside me. He told me where I am, and how I came here. You have done well, Jilly—you and Beorc. I will not forget it."

"Hsst. You must not talk too much. Have you had food?"

"Grimulf has gone to fetch it. Gruel and ale!" He grimaced. "Invalid's fare! I would grow stronger on meat."

"You shall have meat when you are better. When we can provide it. This is not the forest," Juliana reminded him with some severity, "where you can kill a deer whenever it suits you! Gytha must buy our meat, and there is scarce any to be had—"

"Peace, little dragon, I will eat whatever is given me. In truth, I am too thirsty to feel much hunger. And my head is like to crack open."

"Poor brother! The fever has hurt you worse than the

arrow. You are gaunt as a woods-spider. Here is Grimulf with the gruel. I know it is hateful, but eat every bite!"

With the cooling of the fever Sweyn became Sweyn again, and a model invalid, bearing his painful dressing-changes in silence, ready to do whatever he was told. But Juliana soon found the source of his docility was his unchanged determination to get away.

"The sooner I am fit again, the sooner I ride north," he said one morning, waving away her apologies for hurting him.

"But you must rest here for weeks yet! Gain strength and flesh—"

"Nonsense. A se'n-night more will see me mended. Ten days at most. Do you think this the first wound I ever suffered?"

"I do not, then—I have seen the scars on your shoulder and that long one on your thigh. Is it your wish to collect them on every inch of you?"

"It is my wish to ride north and join my companions! You did not think I would stay here, while they fight on?"

After a moment Juliana said with difficulty, "No, I did not think that," though she realized that, unacknowledged, the hope had grown. She lighted a fresh rushlight from the old one, thrust it into the holder, and went to fetch cool water from the well. "What is this—great gathering Beorc spoke of?"

"We are calling up an army for the Aetheling! The word has gone out to Sussex, Wessex, Kent. By summer the north will be full of us. Then Earl Morcar and Earl Edwin will ride to York with their households and their guards . . . It is said the King of Scotland will send an invading force! William the Bastard will have his hands full, little sister. This time we'll have England back, you'll see . . ."

Juliana listened, wondering why she did not kindle with an answering fire, why her heart sank as she remembered the passive young earls on their ponies, the child who was Aetheling—and the grim, dark man riding ahead under his leopard banner, wearing Harold's crown. If there had been a Harold to gather the *fyrds* again, a Harold to confront William like a strong face in a mirror—ah, then! . . . But Harold was twice dead.

"I wish you good fortune," she said desperately.

He looked at her. "And do not believe in it."

"How can I? How can I? Every thane's lands gone, Normans everywhere—"

"What has happened to you, Jilly? Last time we met you begged to ride with me."

"Much good that did me," she remarked. "Sweyn, stay in Canterbury! You could find—work to do—a life to live—"

"I have work to do and a life to live."

"But do you not see yours will kill you, soon or late?"

"So be it—a life to lose. It makes little difference, my sister. I do what I must do."

She gave up, and left him, Wulfric's voice in her mind: *Sweyn is throwing his away.*

F I F T E E N

WULFRIC WAS AS MUCH IN EVIDENCE AS HE DARED WHILE Sweyn's wound mended, drifting over to Stour Street in the free hour after lessons, sometimes foregoing his school supper to share Sweyn's ale and bread. Juliana would not allow him to share the fat hen Gytha had got somehow from the poultry woman under a Norman nose, or the skinny rabbit the butcher's boy had snared. Upstairs they did not eat as well, but nobody commented, nobody cared. Now and again Averil or Bernadette would steal down the outside stair and through the lower doorway under cover of dusk to speak to their old companion; Lady Edwina, attentive briefly but daily to Grimulf, appeared otherwise unaware that her storerooms held anything but stores. And Sweyn, safe as a fox in its earth, mended swiftly, once he had begun.

"Have you told him of our mother?" Wulfric asked Juliana

one evening as they started down the stairs to Sweyn's dark refuge.

"I have not, then! I dare not, Wulf—it would bring the fever back!"

"That's fool's talk. He's no baby. Tell him—or I will."

"You will not, then! Wait a while, I beg you. Till he's better."

"He's better now. You ninny, Easter's a fortnight behind us! She might turn up here any day."

"Any day?" Juliana halted abruptly just inside the arched doorway, dismay flooding over her. She had put the bishop, her mother, the rumored marriage into a far corner of her mind, to devote herself wholly to embroidery and Sweyn. Now she realized that time had not stood still. "But maybe it is not true, Wulf!"

"And maybe it is." Wulfric pushed her aside and walked past her. "I'll say it, if you like."

"No! I will, if we must."

But when she had done so, stammering it out so reluctantly that at last Sweyn raised up on his elbow and demanded what she was trying to say, he did not react with the violence she had been fearing. Instead he went still all over, his face blank and hard, then slowly sank back on his bolster.

"You are not surprised," Wulfric said after a moment.

"Nor would you be, if you but think a little." Sweyn's voice was bitter, but calm enough. He had been quicker than she, Juliana realized, to ask himself if this had been fated since their mother's Norman childhood—if it might be God's will. Certainly it was in her nature to turn to

203

Robert fitzRobert, as it was in theirs to turn away. "When will she come here—she and her baron?" he asked next.

"We do not know that," Wulfric told him. "But come they must, if they mean to take Jilly back to Winchester. She would not go with Lustwin."

"Nor will I go with our mother!" whispered Juliana.

Sweyn's gray eyes turned to her, lingered, and softened even as his wry smile pulled at his face. "I wish you good fortune," he retorted, and whether he quoted her to taunt or hearten she had no chance to ask, for he went on, "You must never tell her you have seen me."

"Sweyn! How can I not? I will, I must!"

He raised up again, his expression suddenly fierce. "I forbid it! Tell her I am dead."

"How can you ask that?" Juliana demanded hotly. "Our own mother! I could not look her in the face and speak such lies!"

Wulfric put in, "It would be cruel."

"It would be crueler to give her hope. Do you think I will let you set the hounds on my trail—on the trail of my companions? I want your silence—and your word on it."

After a moment Juliana looked away, feeling as though she could not speak. At last she said, "And if she asks?"

"Then tell her," said Sweyn gently, "that you know nothing of where I am or whether I am alive or dead. Very soon, that will be true."

After that, the daily possibility of her mother's appearance in Canterbury hung over Juliana like a fog that refused to clear. She was no longer doubtful of Sweyn's recovery;

every evening now she found him out of his bed, prowling the storerooms like a restless shadow, flexing his shoulders and putting a strain on the barely scabbed tear across his back. He was not yet strong enough for the journey ahead of him, but the instant he felt so, he would be gone, she knew that, and she dreaded it as much as her mother's coming. It seemed to her that not even in Hastings had she felt so at the mercy of others, and so helpless to defend herself from whatever blow must fall. Only at the embroidery frame did the day smooth into a pattern of continuity and purpose, of skill and work. The inked lines that became lively faces under her needle, the gesturing hands, the horses with their tensely lifted forelegs, the tunics and cloaks and castles that grew rich with detail, became a private, absorbing world from which she emerged reluctantly at day's end to face the threatening real one.

She tried to imagine a life in Winchester—a life without Wulfric and Canterbury, without the great hanging—and it was chill and empty. She tried to imagine the baron's hall, sitting at table each day with Normans, and was ready to throw in her lot with Sweyn. But she did not know how to escape that life, that hall, with both mother and baron ranged against her.

Inevitably the day came—a Saturday in mid-April, and the hour—mid-afternoon, and the moment when footsteps sounded on the stone steps leading up to the workroom, and she glanced up from the needle she was threading to see Rufus, one of the older novices under Edgar's care at Christ Church Priory, diffidently opening the door. His gaze swept over the faces and found hers. It lingered only an instant, but told her much. As he crossed the room to speak to Brother Adam she was already thrusting her needle into the linen to secure it, pushing back her stool. Her throat had tightened as if hands had closed around it, but she faced the boy steadily enough as he tip-toed over to her, muttering, "Brother Edgar has sent me to fetch you. Your mother is in Canterbury. Brother Adam says you may take what time you need."

Silently Juliana stood up, flicked a glance of thanks toward Brother Adam, who smiled and nodded at her, silently followed Rufus out. She dared not look at Lady Edwina, at Bernadette. They knew nothing of her mother save that she was in Winchester. Since that first day, they had not asked. Knowing well that her Norman kinsman lived in Winchester, they had not needed to. But now?

I should have spoken to them before this, Juliana was thinking as she walked beside Rufus through the pale April sunlight, as unaware of her surroundings as she was of him. Maybe they could have helped me—Lady Edwina would have wanted to help me. Now there is no chance to explain . . . What will I say if my mother asks about Sweyn? We gave him our word, Wulfric and I—yet here he still is, and I know very well whether he is alive or dead! I will have to lie or break oath. I cannot betray Sweyn. Can I look in my mother's eyes and say I know nothing? I must. I will, I suppose . . .

Only another few days and Sweyn would have been gone from Canterbury. She had known that yesterday, when she groped her way through the storerooms at dusk and found him with his peddler's pack propped against the bolster,

206

its contents spread on the bed. She had been dimly conscious of that worn leathern pouch, flung into a dark corner, all this anxious time, but had never asked herself what was inside beside a change of clothing, perhaps a knife. Now she saw peddler's wares as well—a length of lacework, a packet of tanner's bark, a drinking horn and two horn spoons, a braid of candlewick, three cuttlefish bones and horsetail weed for scouring, a pen-mending knife, a good needle in a case. And—something small glinted in the wavering glow of the rushlight—half of a worn silver penny, with old King Edward's face clipped clean across. She picked it up with an exclamation.

"Sweyn! Remember the half penny our father used to carry? He found it once in a horse-trough, and always said it brought him good fortune . . . this is so like."

"It is the same," Sweyn told her. "He gave it to me the morning—before the battle. It was my first battle, you know. And his last," he added bleakly.

"Yeh-so," Juliana whispered. She rubbed a fingertip over the silver half-circle as she had done many a time past, leaning as a little maid against Baldric's leather-bound leg as he told of the lucky finding. For a moment she could almost hear his voice, clear and hearty, often with laughter underneath, could almost feel his strong, hard hands lifting her to his shoulder. She tossed the half penny to the bed again, gesturing to the other objects spread out there.

"Is this your mask for travel, then?"

"More than a mask—my wares. I buy and sell like an honest peddler until it suits me to vanish. It is a good way to enter a town—with the salters and tinkers and poultry women heading for the marketplace. And I go out the gates along with them."

"And does this mean . . . you will soon be going out some Canterbury gate?"

"It does." As she stood in silence, staring at the array on the bed and longing to beg him again to stay, to live, she suddenly found her chin grasped firmly and her face turned to his. "Remember your oath."

"I will, then!" She pulled away. "You need not fear! I will go and tell Grimulf to fetch your supper."

So she had left him yestereve, half-angry, blinking away the helpless tears, knowing that some evening when she came home he would be gone.

But he was not gone yet, she thought as she walked beside Rufus down Burh Street toward the priory—and her mother had come.

"Does Wulfric know?" she asked Rufus suddenly.

"Yeh-so. Brother Edgar sent a boy to Iron Bar Lane when he sent me for you."

He is doubtless there already, thought Juliana. There? Where? Most of the buildings of Christ Church Priory were still blackened wrecks. Mass was said in the former frater-house; the old dormitory served for everything else. There was no longer a guesthall, nor was there an abbot's house, with its own kitchens and guest quarters—no longer room for guests at all.

"Where is my mother?" asked Juliana.

"In the sacristy—there is a little anteroom where the Brothers may receive a visitor—a poor place it is, but . . ."

"Did you—see her? And the man with her? Is he . . . ?"

Is he dark and harsh and confident and proud, will he sweep aside my wishes, override my mother . . . ? She did not know what she wanted to ask, even why she needed to ask. He was a Norman baron.

But Rufus said only, "I saw no one but Brother Edgar. Here—to the right, inside the gate, we must walk around the fallen stones of the church. Mind your footing."

The sacristy was a mere walled-off section of the former dorter, its anteroom smaller and more makeshift yet. Juliana was conscious only of a grouping of men around a woman in a pale headrail who rose abruptly at sight of her, gasped out some exclamation, then rushed forward to fold her in a convulsive embrace. She gladly returned the embrace, but with a sense of confusion. She had certainly expected her mother to enfold her; she had known exactly how it would feel—but it did not feel as it always had. She had grown taller than her mother in these eighteen months. It was now she who stooped slightly to return the kiss, who looked slightly down to meet the ever-anxious, now tear-filled eyes.

"My Juliana," Hildegund quavered, and her voice echoed the confusion Juliana had felt. "So tall! So comely. Is it indeed you? I weep for joy, my daughter, nothing else! I cannot believe I see you standing here . . ."

"Nor I, Mother . . ." Juliana drew a long breath, wrenched her gaze away from the familiar-unfamiliar face in the pale headcloth—it was not only lower, it was a little plumper than she remembered, the gray eyes even larger—and darted a fearful glance toward the men in the room. There were only four, after all; one was Wulfric—

watching her with what seemed stunned speculation. She suddenly realized he was taller, too, near the height of Edgar, who stood next to him. Beside Edgar were two strangers, both richly dressed, one old, one middle-aged. Her glance clung to the latter an instant, in dread—it was a proud face, austere—then shied away back to her mother, who was still talking to her.

"Wulfric has told me of your journey! My lambs! So hard-pressed, nothing to eat . . . you should have gone to your uncle, my Juliana! Indeed, Wulfric should not have run away from the good Brothers to look for you—"

"God knows it is as well he did! Or I surely would *not* be standing here," said Juliana absently. Her thoughts were hurrying their own anxious ways. Wulfric had plainly said nothing of Sweyn or the camp in the forest—but soon there must come a direct question. "My mother—" she began, not knowing what she would say, only that she must say something to stave off the moment. "Will you not . . . will you not sit down—"

Again she flicked a wary look toward the austere stranger. As she did so he turned to face the older man, and she saw his tonsure—and suddenly knew him for the prior.

"I will leave you, Baron," he was saying. "You will wish to speak privily. Lady, pray make what use you need of this room, it is yours until nightfall. Brother Edgar, you are excused from vespers . . ."

Juliana was dimly aware of voices replying, of farewells, of the prior's leaving. She was staring past him, unbelieving, at the face of her mother's new husband—a gentle, elderly face, its forehead crossed with wrinkles, its cheeks

210

deeply grooved below mild brown eyes, the head thrust a little forward above a tall, stooped frame that seemed to be apologizing for its presence. And at last her mother was drawing her forward.

"My Juliana—here is Baron Geoffrey fitzJohannes, long a friend of your uncle's. And now my husband."

Juliana found herself bowing her head, bending a knee slightly, as she had been taught as a little maid, murmuring something through lips gone stiff and cold. The baron was bowing, too, with sober grace.

"I have long awaited this meeting, Daughter of my Lady." His voice was deep, a little rusty—an old man's voice; his gray-streaked hair touched his collar in the Saxon way. As indeed, so had their uncle's, always. This was not one of William's Normans, but one of old King Edward's —though a Norman, still. "Please to sit down with your mother," he added gravely.

He moved away toward Edgar with a courtier's tact and ease, as Juliana obeyed him. Wulfric—his stunned expression now fully explained—came to sit on the other side of their mother, trying to catch Juliana's eye. She met his briefly, wondering if her expression was a mirror of his own.

"And now, my lambs, you must tell me everything—"

But it seemed Hildegund had already heard much, from the visiting bishop who brought back news of them to Winchester, from Edgar while they were being fetched from school and workroom, from Wulfric before Juliana arrived. Mechanically Juliana answered courteous queries about Lady Edwina's health, about Averil and Bernadette, about the embroidery, brushed aside anxious ones about her early, difficult days in Canterbury, asked after Nurse Editha and Lustwin and Ragni.

"All are well, my dear, and you will scarce know Ragni —she is eager to see you! But . . ." Hildegund's eyes were filling again. "I know nothing of Sweyn. I have asked everywhere. I fear he fell in the battle, with your father . . ." Her voice trailed off, her gaze grew suddenly intent. "Juliana! Do you know different?"

Realizing her face must have betrayed her, Juliana said, "He did not fall in the battle, Mother. I saw him two days after. He was wounded, not dead. But he made me leave him—and then I was captured."

"But afterwards? Now?" exclaimed her mother.

The moment had come. She dared not look at Wulfric, but met her mother's eyes. "That was months ago. I know no more than you of where he is now, or whether he is alive or dead."

"He lives! I must believe it. Somewhere he lives! Oh, why did he not come to Winchester, to safety—"

"He would not do that, Mother," said Juliana.

"Maybe he could not," Wulfric hastened to put in.

"No. He would not," Hildegund said slowly, sadly. "He was ever at odds with your uncle . . ."

There was a silence, then she looked again at Juliana, who could follow her thought as if she had spoken it.

"As I was, too," Juliana said. "Nor will I go to Winchester, Mother. I wish to stay here."

It was done. The lie had been spoken, her stand taken, all in the same few moments. And the battle was now joined—so quickly she knew her mother had expected it.

"Now, my daughter! What are you saying! Of course you must come home with me—how can it be otherwise? You must do as I tell you. Baron—"

She stretched a hand toward her husband, who came to her quickly. Juliana, reminded irresistibly of other days, of childhood arguments over garments or ponies and Nurse Editha's decisive intervention, got to her feet to face him.

Instead of direct command, she received soft words. "Daughter of my Lady, your mother is over-anxious. It is too soon, my dear, to speak of all that. Tell your daughter of our plans, our hopes. Come, I will sit with you. Brother Edgar, join us . . ."

"I have my own plans," said Juliana, and remained standing.

Edgar said, "My dear Juliana, do your mother the courtesy of hearing her out!"

And to her surprise, Wulfric, too, said, "Sit down, Jilly." Somewhat enigmatically, he added, "It will make no difference."

Juliana sat down. Her mother's plans and hopes were exactly what she expected. She was to accompany them at once to the Canterbury house where they were staying with old friends of the baron; tomorrow they would attend Mass and afterwards call on Lady Edwina. On the day following the morrow, they must set out for Rochester, where the baron had kinsmen, and afterwards journey on to London and then Westminster, in good time for the crowning of Lady Matilda as Queen on Whitsunday. After the festivities—home to Winchester.

"I wish you a good journey," said Juliana. "But I will stay here, with Wulfric. My home is in Canterbury."

"Now Juliana! Your home is with us! You are my daughter!"

"I am also my father's daughter! And nothing can change it."

There was a brief silence. "That—that is true, certainly!" Hildegund faltered. "But no one is trying to change it! You will see, my child . . . You must not let foolish prejudice—"

"My dear," the baron broke in. "I am a yet a stranger to your daughter. It is too soon to discuss this."

"No doubt it is. Now, my lamb! Now, you must heed the baron, and not say yea or nay so soon. You must see the gifts I have brought you! A fine mantle—sky-blue, with an embroidered border—a silver pin for your shoulder . . . Come now with us to the house where we are staying! Our host is the knight Vital, whose father was long the baron's friend—"

"The knight Vital?" exclaimed Juliana. Her gaze flew to Edgar, whose sober features had frozen. "But—but do you not know—that house was the home of Edgar's mother's kin? God's mercy, they were turned out into the street that Bishop Odo might give it to his favorite! I will never step into that house—nor the house of any Norman!"

There was an instant's shocked silence, then Edgar got to his feet—clumsily, as if they had frozen, too—and bowed first to Hildegund, then to the baron. "Forgive me," he murmured. "I have matters to attend to." He left the room.

"Oh, may St. Agnes help me, what have I done!" cried Hildegund.

Wulfric said drily, "You have chosen the wrong house to stay in."

"But Wulfric—! We were invited—indeed, he seemed most gracious—"

"My Lady's Daughter, I beg you will believe me—" the baron's voice shook a little. "This knight's father was my friend—I have not seen the son since he was a young boy . . . I would never—it was not intentional . . ."

Plainly, they had blundered in ignorance, were appalled by the consequences, and were only now realizing how unwelcome to their Saxon family was their coming. The baron's furrowed face was drawn with strain. He had risen when Edgar did; now he glanced toward the door as if he would willingly have removed his intrusive person but for the need to stand by his wife. Juliana, sitting stiff and angry, listened to their fragmented apologies, saw the emotional disarray into which she had cast them, and felt her own hostility relax. She was suddenly certain that there was no way on earth their will could be imposed on hers.

"My mother," she said, "can you not see that all has changed—that everything is different—that *I* am different from when we last met? I cannot go back into your household. I will not. I pray you, be content with Ragni, who is a little maid and will do as you bid, and live the life you wish for her."

"But, my love, I wish only for you to take your rightful place! Here, you are neither wed nor betrothed nor yet the birth-daughter of the Lady whose house you share . . . you labor at needlework for coins, not pastime! It is such a strange life."

"But it is mine. It is the one I found for myself, and indeed, it does not seem strange to me. I have friends, I have kin, I live in a Saxon household. I am needed—to work on the great hanging. I would work on it gladly without the coins! In Canterbury, I am . . . more than the daughter of my mother."

"Oh, you were ever a willful child—!"

"My lady, I think your daughter is no longer a child," the baron told her gently. "Come, it will be better to sleep on this decision. Tell me, do you not feel we should find Brother Edgar and speak to him?"

As Hildegund turned to him with what was plainly relief, the vesper bells clanged distantly from the abbey, and soon from nearby came the tinkling of the handbell that was all the priory had left to ring. Juliana glanced at Wulfric and found him watching her with a half-smile. The battle was over. There remained only the task of making their mother accept defeat.

The bells gave a welcome signal to the four of them to leave the sacrister's little anteroom and go their separate ways. Juliana arranged to meet her mother outside the abbey church on the morrow. "We will go together to Mass. I will ask Brother Alain if I may show you the embroidery. Then maybe you will understand . . . And I will ask Lady Edwina if I may bring you to call on her in the afternoon. Forgive me, but I cannot invite the baron." She turned to him, met his eyes. "It is Lady Edwina's house, and no Norman is welcome in it."

He bowed in silence, she and Wulfric kissed their mother, and they parted. But outside the gates, when she turned to take her leave of Wulfric, he said, "I'm coming with you." He did not speak again until they were crossing Burh Street into Mercery Lane—now almost deserted,

216

with the ending of Saturday's market-day. Then he glanced at her and shrugged. "He is not, after all, so bad, that baron."

After a reluctant moment, she said, "No."

"I see well why our uncle chose him to look after her."

"Yeh-so. I see, too."

"He would never be dragging you away from here. I think he would as soon not have you with them." Wulfric gave a little bark of laughter. "I cannot blame him. As well have a burr under the saddle." They turned into High Street, dodged past the merchants putting up their shutters, passed the empty pillory. "You will tell Sweyn you are bringing her to Stour Street tomorrow," he said a bit anxiously.

"Certainly I will tell him. Also that I kept my oath! But it will be hard tomorrow, sitting in the room upstairs with all of us—save only our mother—knowing who is hiding below! *Sweyn* is hard, not to see her for just a moment. It was hard to lie to her."

"Come, Jilly. You know well our mother could never keep her tongue between her teeth. You had to lie."

But when they reached the storeroom, they found that Juliana had after all spoken truth. Sweyn was gone. The straw bed was stripped and empty, the peddler's pack had vanished. Grimulf, emerging out of the shadows, said he had glimpsed him on King's Bridge an hour past, mingling with the tinkers and the salters, bound for the town gates at the end of the market day.

"I could scarce tell him from the others, Thane's Daughter. He'll get where he's going."

Wherever that was. From now on, in truth, they would know nothing of him, or whether he was alive or dead.

Grimulf dug into the leather pouch at his waist and brought something out. "He left these for you."

To Wulfric he handed the little knife for sharpening pens that Juliana had seen among the peddler's wares. Into her own hand dropped a bit of something shiny she had to peer at through her tears.

It was her father's silver half-penny. Sweyn was saying "Good fortune"—and goodbye.

EPILOGUE

TWO MORNINGS LATER, HILDEGUND AND HER BARON AND
their entourage left Canterbury on their leisurely way to
Westminster and the coronation. Juliana, standing with
Wulfric to watch the horses pass through Westgate in the
early sunlight, was conscious of mingled feelings of homesickness and relief, and of a new freedom that put her very
much on her mettle. She had won it—but what she did
with it was up to her.

The Sunday had gone reasonably well. Hildegund had
seen the work in progress on the great hanging—as had
Wulfric, who had seized the chance to be first of the school
to look upon it. Juliana had received her gifts. Later they
had called on Brother Odbold and seen Wulfric's scribing,
later still supped with Lady Edwina and her daughters in
the house in Stour Street.

Somehow, during the day, Hildegund had grown reconciled to her daughter's strange life—whether because of old deference to Lady Edwina's opinions, or the persuadings of her new husband, Juliana never knew. And now this morning, as the horses disappeared behind their own cloud of dust, and she and Wulfric turned from Westgate to walk back in thoughtful silence through the bustle of the town, she found she had forgiven her mother for marrying a Norman—now that she had met the Norman and understood.

She also, with some reluctance, decided to forgive the baron for his birth. It was not, after all, a thing he could say yea or nay to, and he had lived in southern England all his life. So long as she did not have to share his household or heed his advice, he might live, and care for her mother, with her good will.

The weeks of springtime passed, varied with sun and rain, filled with embroidery and walks with Wulfric and feast days with Bernadette and Leifsi and Goldwin. Edgar and the others of the priory lived by their Rule as best they could in their burnt-out ruins, hoping for a new archbishop. Wulfric scribed on, undaunted. At St. Augustine's, the abbot, Father Aethelsige, was found one morning to have fled into Denmark, escaping perhaps from Earl Odo's ill will, perhaps from King William's. His duties lay heavy on the dean and his absence on all the Brothers. But the change was not allowed to affect the workroom or the great hanging, where the spindles continued to rise and fall, the needles to go in and out, and the figures to spring into life and color on the linen.

When a new abbot was appointed, he was Norman.

Juliana's new tolerance toward the baron did not extend to the new abbot, or King William, or Lord Devil, or Norman knights who lived in Saxon halls, or the soldiers whose great, tall horses crowded her off the road, or any Normans who had sailed in striped ships—nor to their wives. As summer came, and wore away, these were appearing in Canterbury in increasing numbers, bringing children and creating a sharp demand for nursemaids. Rosamond, once thread girl for the workroom, now the wife of a Canterbury mercer, spent her afternoons in such service to offset the Norman taxes which grew heavier every month. Encountering her in Mercery Lane one Saturday, Juliana saw the two children she was minding, heard them talking to her in a mingling of Norman and Saxon words, and wondered whose language they would wind up speaking.

She herself closed her ears to Norman speech wherever she heard it, and remained as obstinately Saxon as she could. One dealt as one was able with a conqueror's heel, she reflected one afternoon as her needle traced the outline of a castle. Her father had died fighting it; Harold had let God judge, and died as well. Rhonwen made use of it to climb to freedom; Lady Edwina chose to forget it; Brother Alain bowed, when he had to, to its commands. Her mother had made a separate peace with it; Sweyn would be ground under it, battling to the death. Wulfric alone had not let it deflect him from what he had always meant to do.

As for herself, she clung to Saxon ways in a land no longer Saxon, a life no longer ordered or even certain. It sometimes seemed as though Normans filled the world. But she

221

knew there were thousands of others like herself, slowly finding the shape of their changed lives, poorer and shabbier and harder-pressed but clinging fast to old, stubborn words and customs, no matter who took the taxes.

She straightened up from the linen, thrust her needle in and half-out to hold it, and rubbed her fingertips, which were sore from an hour of outline stitch. As she massaged them, her gaze moved from her own unfinished castle to the mounted spearmen galloping into Brittany under the hands of Christiana and Brother Adam, then to the ink-line drawings pegged around the walls. Brother Alain had completed the designs now, to the end of the story. The pale brown lines traced Norman horses charging up Caldbec Hill, arrows flying, Saxons standing crowded behind their shields. And below in the border slain men and beasts lay stripped and dismembered, forever stilled. She could almost hear the flies. It was truth he was drawing. And at the end was William, on Harold's throne. That, too, was truth.

The hanging seemed to her a great work; maybe as great as the one depicting the Battle of Maldon that Lady Edwina had seen once, which had been embroidered a hundred years ago. It seemed a worthy work to spend one's days on. And maybe this one, too, would last a hundred years.

Meanwhile the Aetheling had fled to Scotland; rebels and William's men clashed repeatedly in the north, and word filtered back of Norman castles rising in Warwick and Nottingham and York and Lincoln and Cambridge—as they rose, here, in rich color on linen, in this sunny workroom.

She plucked out her needle and bent once more over

the linen. She no longer believed the rebels would take back England. She had long ceased to wish she might fight beside Sweyn. Men were still dying and halls going up in flames and there was nothing she could do about it. The world was as it was. But she thought she had finally found her place. It was here in Canterbury, sharing the private world of the great embroidery with these few others, and changing her nightmare memories into thread.

A F T E R W O R D

THE GREAT EMBROIDERED HANGING KNOWN AS THE BAY-
eux Tapestry has lasted not a mere hundred years, as Juliana
hoped, but more than nine hundred. In this, as in many
ways, it is unique—the only remaining example of an art
form fairly common in the early Middle Ages. We have
records in old chronicles of other such works, for example
the one depicting the Battle of Maldon, but the hangings
themselves have long since vanished.

Nobody knows who designed the Bayeux Tapestry, what
hands embroidered it, or even—for sure—where it was
made. But various clues point to England, to Canterbury,
even to St. Augustine's Abbey; and the prominence given
in the scenes and inscriptions to King William's half-
brother, Bishop Odo, and certain of his favorites (such as
the knights Vital and Wadard) strongly suggest that Odo
had something to do with it. There is good evidence that
it was created some time in the dozen years following the
Conquest; during those years Odo was master of all Kent,
active in Canterbury affairs and also building a church in
Bayeux, where he was bishop.

The Bayeux embroidery is just under twenty inches high
and two hundred thirty feet long, embroidered in wool on
linen. It was originally a little longer; the final scene, which
undoubtedly showed William crowned and on his throne,
is missing.

For six and a half centuries it was kept in the Church of

Notre-Dame of Bayeux. Each year it was brought out and hung around the nave of the church during the Feast of Relics—perhaps the same relics Harold's oath was sworn on. Afterwards it was rolled up and put away again. Its existence was unsuspected by the rest of France.

Then, in the early 1700's, a few curious Frenchmen heard of it and pursued the clues. Eventually a set of drawings was made of parts of it. It was after this that its life became perilous. During the French Revolution it narrowly escaped being used as pack-cloth to cover wagons. Two years later it was barely prevented from being cut in pieces to decorate a float during a public holiday. Napoleon recognized it as a national treasure and turned it over to the state, but for the next fifty years it was transferred here and there, kept wound on two cylinders which damaged the linen every time it was unwound, and nobody seemed to be in charge. It was not until the end of World War II that the tapestry was returned to Normandy from its last storage place in Paris. It now has a whole building, the former Grand Seminaire, as a permanent place of exhibition, in Bayeux, France.

The work is faded and stained in spots, and much mended—hardly surprising in the passage of nine hundred years. But it still glows with life; horses gallop, wind fills the striped sails, men fight and work and ride with a vitality seldom matched in any work of art. And it remains the most direct source of information in existence about the clothes, the armor, the weapons and ships and people of the time, and about the still-mysterious figure of Harold Godwinson and the events preceding the Norman Conquest.

G L O S S A R Y

Aetheling: The crown prince, heir to the throne. In 1066 this was Edward, the young nephew of King Edward the Confessor.

bailey: a large, walled enclosure, part of the typical Norman castle complex, around which were ranged the stables, the storerooms, the guardhouse, etc.

bertha: a division of Canterbury in Saxon times, roughly corresponding to the later *wards.*

boggart: an evil creature, a bogie-man.

bogle: another word for the *boggart.*

braies: men's loose breeches, often to the ankle and wrapped from ankle to knee with strips of cloth or leather.

burgh: the dwelling and enclosed grounds of a Saxon thane.

embossing: decorating silver or other metal by hammering in patterns so that they will stand out either higher or lower than the original smooth surface.

farmery: the infirmary, or hospital, of a monastery.

folkmoot: an assembly of the people of a town or shire.

fyrd: the Saxon militia, consisting of thanes and the men who owed them service in peace or war.

girdle: a waist belt, usually leather, worn by both men and women, though the woman's was wider.

headrail: a long, wide stole or scarf worn by Saxon married or widowed women over the head and draped around the shoulders, with the ends falling to knee-length.

hides: a *hide* was a measurement of land in Saxon England (excepting Kent), corresponding to the usual holding of one peasant family, the precise size of which varied. Thus the meaning of the term is still elusive.

keep: the main tower of a castle; a stronghold.

kirtle: a floor-length tunic, with a round or V neck and long, close-fitting cuffed sleeves, worn by Saxon women over a chemise shirt-garment. The *kirtle* might be linen or wool.

leman: lover or mistress.

lorimers: makers of spurs, bits, and other hardware for harnesses and horse-trappings.

mantle: a cloak, cut square, either knee-length or to the ground, drawn up in front and fastened with a brooch or tie under the chin or on one shoulder. Men's *mantles* often had hoods attached.

motte: a man-made hill of earth dug out of the ditch (or moat) that encircled it. The castle *keep* was built on top of the *motte,* with a drawbridge across the surrounding ditch to the walled *bailey* spread out on the other side. The ditch often—but not always—contained water.

reeve: the bailiff, or foreman, of a Saxon thane's or nobleman's estate.

rocc: a woman's over-tunic, put on over the head and worn over the *kirtle*. It was cut full and floor-length, and was usually hitched up over the *girdle* to reveal the *kirtle* (often of a different color) underneath. Both *kirtle* and *rocc* were often richly embroidered around the hems, wrists, and neck.

se'n-night: seven nights; that is, one week.

sester: a unit of measure, used for honey, salt, and some other commodities.

simples: homemade remedies, usually herbal.

skep: the type of beehive used in Saxon times (and much later). Usually basketwork, conical in shape, woven of rye straw.

water-nix: an imaginary humanlike spirit, kin to elves and fairies, thought to inhabit streams and woodland brooks.

Weald: the vast forest that once spread over southern England. The word means "forest" in Old English.

witan: or *witan gemot,* the king's council, a sort of parliament of Saxon times, composed of nobles and thanes. It had great power and importance under the Saxon kings, who made few important decisions without consulting it. There was a *witan* for every section of the country—West Saxon, Sussex, Kent, etc.

yeh-so: The Anglo-Saxon word was spelled *gea* but pronounced "yeah," and the usual custom was to add "so." This usage resulted in our modern word "yes."